LIFE
IS A LONG
STORY SHORT

LESSONS
FROM LIVING
THROUGH ABUSE,
ABANDONMENT,
AND ADOPTION

Glenn J. Koster, Sr.

Illustrated By
Beth Boese

WESTBOW
PRESS®
A DIVISION OF THOMAS NELSON
& ZONDERVAN

WestBow Press books may be ordered through booksellers or by contacting:

WestBow Press
A Division of Thomas Nelson & Zondervan
1663 Liberty Drive
Bloomington, IN 47403
www.westbowpress.com
1 (866) 928-1240

ISBN: 978-1-5127-3295-5 (sc)

Library of Congress Control Number: 2016903480

Print information available on the last page.

WestBow Press rev. date: 3/11/2016

Dedicated To

My wife
Charlcie Koster

Who has put up with my storytelling, my poetry,
and untold hours at the computer.

My children
Glenn Jr., Heather, Laura, Matthew, and SkyLee

Who have had to listen to me prattle on when they
had no idea what I was really trying to say.

My parents
George & Ruth Koster

Who taught me so much of what I have learned in life.
My Dad passed away in February 2015
before the final draft was complete.

Acknowledgements

An effort of this magnitude is one that cannot be accomplished in a vacuum, which means that I have a host of people to thank! While gratitude is due to the myriad people who have listened to my stories, read them (sometimes more than once), or proofread them, special thanks have to go out to several people.

All of the illustrations included in this book are the work of **Beth Boese**, who I met through my wife. She is a very talented artist, whose renderings for my short stories were not influenced by me in any way. As she read each story, the words became alive in the vision she had for each accompanying illustration. I will be forever grateful for her inspiration, talent, and encouragement!

A special thank you is reserved for **Robb Reeves** who has put up with me as a reporter, a columnist, and a friend. Robb has helped me hone my writing skills even when he was not aware of his involvement. His encouragement has been invaluable, but not only on this book but also in agreeing to publish my monthly column, *The Prairie Tattler*, which runs the fourth week of every month in the Harvey County Independent (Halstead, KS).

Special thanks have to go **Temple Miller**, a college friend of my wife's, who agreed to edit the rough draft of this book. While her guidance was invaluable in clarifying what I wanted to say, her grammatical corrections of my words were much appreciated.

A final word of thanks has to go to my wife, **Charlcie Koster**, for putting up with me these many months while I labored over this work. During this time I worked a full-time job during the day and another part-time gig as a reporter for the Independent. As a result, my free time around the house has been limited and she has graciously picked up the slack. In addition, she has offered encouragement and proofreading. Along the way, she also took every opportunity to make my stories more widely known by sharing them both through email and public readings for the folks who attend Young At Heart in Hutchinson, Bunco, and Red Hats.

Thank you – every one of you!

Contents

Foreword

Glenn Koster is a writer for my newspaper. Eight years after meeting him, he asked me to read his manuscript and write the foreword. As I read, my view of Glenn changed. Before reading his stories, Glenn was a news writer, someone I relied on to provide the paper with content.

The more I read, the more I realized Glenn was inspirational with a breadth of personal experiences.

This book is about a man's stories. We all collect stories and they are meant to be told.

Our stories are an efficient and powerful way to communicate. Some stories are funny. Many are sad. Some spark action within. And all are told so that we can relate to someone better. We hope by telling a story, the listener learns more about himself and us.

When you read Glenn's stories, his words seep into you, making you think about others and with the realization we think too much about us. We are at our best when we help people. That is a common thread in this book. So is God's love and his ability to give us hope and encouragement.

My favorite story in this collection is *No Place To Turn*. The inspiration for it came when Glenn experienced a cold night in Denver. In *No Place To Turn* you feel the winter air cut into a newly homeless family. They are living and shivering in their car and you see their desperation. The children know something is wrong and may even understand they have no home.

The story ends with Christian love. Members of a church provide the family with income and shelter. It is a happy ending.

This book is about happy endings, which are possible when we look out for our neighbors. We need stories like the ones in this book; we need to help each other.

Glenn Koster took the time to write down his stories and I hope his words inspire action in others. That is what good stories do.

Robb Reeves,
Publisher
Harvey County Independent

Preface

All of these stories are based on real life experiences, either from my life or in the lives of people that I have known. Life is a long story, with twists and turns at points we frequently do not expect. When we think we finally have life figured out, time and again we find we have to start all over again. The inspirations gleaned from the lives of others are often vital resources during life's struggles.

Yet all of these pieces are short stories. In fact, most are truly short-short stories from 750 to 1,000 words, and they are designed to teach basic principles of Christian faith. I do not seek to imbue the reader with esoteric tales intended to teach deep theological thought. Rather, my aim is to start at the basics – not only for those just learning to walk with Christ but also as refreshers for those who have walked a lifetime.

My love for writing began early in my life, often as an escape from the realities that I faced. My birth father was a disabled Korean War POW, who had an abysmal time keeping any sort of job. Consequently, we lived in abject poverty. Imagine a one-room log cabin with six kids and two adults and you have a picture of our family.

Unfortunately, poverty was not the only aspect of living I sought to escape. My father was abusive, in many ways. As his oldest, I often caught the brunt of his physical abuse, which was truly just the tip of the iceberg.

When I was six, my folks left to seek a better life, ostensibly leaving me in the care of my aunt who never showed. Abandoned. My two older half-brothers and I were able to survive in rural Michigan for some weeks on our own. How three boys, ages six, seven, and nine, subsisted is still unimaginable, but we succeeded.

Eventually someone caught on to our plight and rescued us, in the loosest sense of the word. Custody was awarded to my aunt who had not shown up, and who still really did not want the responsibility. After trial and error at the hands of the Michigan courts, we were pulled from my aunt's home. The father of my older brothers traveled back to Michigan to claim them, but since I was not a blood relative of their father he was denied any claim to my fate. I was the odd man out as no one else came to claim me.

I was placed for adoption, but it proved to be an experiment that went awry. I did not fare much better there than with my birth family and was pulled from that home a short 13 months later and moved miles away.

My first foster experience blissfully passed until a fateful December day in 1964. After a joyous Christmas shopping excursion, my foster father laid down on the sofa when we arrived home. During the night, he passed away.

Back through the system I went, I spent time in two different foster homes before being re-adopted. The second time around was a rousing success!

However, by this time I had learned two things about life. First, never make a personal connection with anyone if you can avoid it because it makes it easier if things do not work out as planned. Secondly, I learned too that I had to prove I belonged. No matter what I was involved in, I was competitive and driven.

But I also escaped by reading any book I could get my hands on and through writing. Abandoned as a child, abused, and twice adopted, writing was a natural escape. Unfortunately, much of that writing occurred before computers and the Internet and so it has been lost. In recent years, I have taken extra effort to ensure I saved my writings. Alas, technology advances faster than my ability to archive from one machine to another. The result has been the additional loss of a great many stories.

My saga does not end there. As an adult, despite being out of the environment for many years, I had learned enough in childhood that I repeated the mistakes of my birth family. I became abusive. I turned to alcohol. I escaped into work.

In the spring of 1989, after my first marriage of 16 years began to dissolve, I set about making some changes. Yet, in order to make the changes necessary, I had to learn why I had become who I was. What made me the person I had become? I really did not know because the first seven years of my life with the abuse, the poverty, and the neglect were all erased from my mind.

In October of that same year, I made the reconnection – but that is a story for another time. My eyes were opened when I met my birth father. I had become the personification of him. When I met my grandmother the following morning, it was just as revealing. He had grown to learn her ways while growing up, and he repeated them perfectly.

But out of that reconnection (and the one that followed with my mother a month later), the years of keeping my past buried finally gave way to restoration, relief, and full recovery.

What does one do under such circumstances? How can I best get my story out in a way that I can help as many people as possible? Publish!

Indeed, I decided writing and sharing my life stories the best avenue. I would tell the stories gleaned from my life of wandering and recovery and the stories assembled from watching others experience life.

I have been through a great deal in my life, and it has taught me much. Hopefully, by sharing what I have learned and observed, I will be able to provide hope to others who struggle with their faith, their lives, and their families.

I have also become an observer, which serves me well in my part-time career as a reporter for a variety of Kansas newspapers. I see things that most people never even notice.

Of course, these traits left me with another dilemma. What would I use as a title and how would I organize a hodgepodge of short stories? The title, "Life is a Long Story Short" seemed a natural fit.

Beth Boese

Be It Resolved
(January)

"Do not conform to the pattern of this world, but be transformed by the renewing of your mind." (Romans 12:2)

Pacing between his desk and the window had become one of Jerome's trademarks. Whenever he was perplexed, or deep in thought, pacing seemed to provide just enough of a relief to ease the mental tension. Pushing his chair back from his desk, Jerome was soon deep in a state of mental anguish, wearing deeper the well-worn groove in the plush blue carpet.

He hated the thought of having to come up with yet another resolution only to see it vanish as quickly as a New Year's Day hangover. He had made and broken enough New Year's resolutions in his life to know that such tasks were always a nuisance, and guaranteed to fail. Yet, every year, Jerome continued to make them. He somewhat figured that he did not have a choice in the matter. Not only did people seem to expect others to make resolutions and break them, but resolutions also were always good for a good guffaw and hearty backslap to begin the most mundane of the early January meetings to which he was subjected.

Maybe it wasn't so much that Jerome disliked making resolutions. This year just seemed so different from all the others.

He had spent most of his early childhood being raised in a proper, Christian home. He had even made a profession of faith in front

1

of the church as a teenager. The church did not hold his interest and during the early stages of his adult life, Jerome drifted away. However, the past year saw a rebirth of the old faith Jerome had clung to as a teenager. Somehow this very fact made things different.

Instead of the usual cavorting about on New Year's Eve, this year found Jerome kneeling before God. Instead of waking up New Year's Day with the typical hangover from one too many glasses of champagne, Jerome woke up with a new energy and a new outlook for the coming year. Half expecting the euphoria to subside with the passage of time, it just seemed to grow. The busy holiday weekend had passed and Jerome felt as energetic and renewed on this his first day back at the office as he had on New Year's morning.

Only one thing remained to be done. He fully expected his boss to go around the room during the usual staff meeting and ask for New Year's resolutions. Jerome had a feeling that the only reason the old coot asked for the resolutions was to have a chance to tear down the poor soul who somehow managed to make it into the new year with optimism. Jerome knew all too well how cutting George could be. He also realized that it was unavoidable. Jerome just had to think up something to say.

The problem was Jerome did not feel like just making a resolution to have something to say. He really did feel that this was going to be a different year. He wanted to make that clear to everyone. But how?

Tap. Tap. Tap. Quietly, Jim rapped on the door and poked his head inside. "You ready?" Jim asked. "You know how much the old man enjoys the first staff meeting each year..."

"*Yes*", thought Jerome, "*everyone knows.*" Turning at look at Jim, Jerome shrugged his shoulders as if to say, "We might as well get it over with."

The small conference room quickly filled with the hum of people in conversation. Jerome and Jim managed to wiggle their way to a back corner. Maybe Jerome could get out of making any public resolutions if he could blend in with the room's décor.

"Good morning." It was George. In typical style, George dressed like an ad out of GQ. He truly lived the slogan dress for success.

"Happy New Year!" George declared. "Okay, I am a couple of days late, but so what? That gave you guys a couple of extra days to try to stick to your resolutions. Anybody have any luck with their resolutions this year?"

As soon as George mentioned the word resolution, you could hear the muffled groans rise from the dozen or so people crammed into the small room. Yet, no one offered a response to George's query.

Undaunted, George charged right in. He singled out several of the clerical staff first. Then, after sufficient suffrage, George turned his attention to the sales staff. Glancing from face to face, George and Jerome's eyes met in a prolonged exchange. "Tell me, Jerome," George began. "What did you come up with this year? Do you have more of the usual stuff about greater sales volumes, customer follow-up and attention to detail? No, let me guess. You got a little more personal this year and resolved to give up your Michelin belly."

The room roared at Jerome's expense.

There was no escape now. Jerome was on the spot and terribly unprepared. Silently, Jerome offered a prayer of desperation. "Please, Lord. Give me the words to say. I have come a long way in the past year. Now I need you to direct my steps – and my tongue."

"I resolved this year to love the Lord with all my heart, my strength, my soul and my mind. I also resolved to truly love my neighbor as myself." As soon as he began his utterance, Jerome felt his heart jump. He did not understand why, but once he started, Jerome just couldn't seem to retract anything. When he finished, the same feeling of euphoria that he had experienced on New Year's Day returned. The butterflies flitted quietly out from his stomach. His confidence returned.

George was stunned. No one had ever dared to share a resolution of faith. Without fanfare and without retort, George shuffled the pile of papers he had prepared for the meeting. With obvious uneasiness, he began to hand out the meeting agenda to those present.

You could have heard a pin drop in the room as the agendas were silently passed from hand to hand. As each person pulled a copy from the top of the pile, you could sense an uneasiness spread across the room. With each passing paper, the pressure mounted. No one was sure what would transpire next. No one sensed what was about to occur would have ever had a chance of happening.

Just as quickly as it had been lost, George's composure returned. "Thank you, Jerome. That took a lot of courage. I appreciate you candor – and the seriousness of the matters that you have resolved to change in your life," George continued. "If there is any way that I can help you stick to your resolutions, I assure you that I will be available. Now, let's get down to business."

Jerome, still flush from embarrassment, smiled. With a new outlook, he truly embraced the resolution he had so quickly muttered. His resolution could only have been supplied by God and could only be honored with God's help. But, yes, it was his resolution and he silently vowed to make this a year for God!

Author's Insight - A New Beginning

A new year is a very frightening thing for some people to face. Each year is often a repeat of the same problems, same job, and the same habits. The experience can be very discouraging if you have no hope of actually making improvements in your life.

Imagine, if you can, what it is like to face every new year with the same agenda before you. You know that you have to change your diet and lose some weight. You have tried, repeatedly, but you have never been able to do anything about it. You are tired and bored with your job, but know full well that you cannot afford to change jobs at this point. You know that your marriage is in need of some help, but help is expensive and time consuming.

A fact of life is that no one seems to have enough time or money. Every year the same problems bring the same resolutions and yield the same results. The outlook can be very discouraging.

As Christians, we have a different message. Instead of discouragement, we have a message of hope to offer the world. We know that each year can be different. Each year can be faced with a sense of purpose and renewal.

We can look to the future with hope because God has provided a message of love and hope. No longer do we have to face each year with just ourselves or close family members to rely on. God has promised that He will be there with us.

There is just one catch. With a message of such importance, the mere fact that we have personal knowledge of this message implants within us a responsibility - and privilege - to carry that message to the world.

A lot has been written and said in the mid-1990s about the message of hope that Princess Diana and Mother Theresa carried to the world. Princess Di offered a message of hope, but it was a temporal hope. Mother Theresa offered a message of eternal hope. Yet, far too often we let others speak that message for us. We have forgotten that God has commanded each and every one of His children to "confess with your mouth the Lord Jesus." This is not an option, but a command.

Yet, the message that we must carry to the world is also a message that we must consider a privilege to deliver. I mention that this is a privilege because each year brings a new lease on the life that God has called us to live. We have been called not to be conformed to this world, but to be transformed.

Imagine a young child with no hope and no parents. When that child experiences the joy of adoption, do you think for a minute that he will be silent? No way! We have been adopted by God, as joint heirs with Christ, and yet we walk about in silence never telling those around us that God offers the same adoption to them.

We can no longer be silent. We must offer to the world the message of hope that God has offered. Our message must be carried, not out of responsibility or command, but out of joy. We are privileged to be loved by God - but so is all of humanity. We must let them know it.

We must make every year a year when we truly live for God in every aspect of our being!

For God
so loved the
world that he gave
his only
begotten
son so
that whoever
believes
in him shall
have everlasting
life
John 3:16

Beth Boese

A Special Love
(February)

*"Do not be yoked together with
unbelievers."(II Corinthians 6:14)*

Kevin raced into the store. Like normal, he was late and didn't have much time to waste. It had been a very busy week. He was due to pick up Laurie in half an hour and he had not even bought a card yet! Quickly picking out a card that expressed his love for Laurie in simple but elegant terms, Kevin paid the clerk and hurried out.

Normally, Valentine's Day was not exactly a holiday that he relished. This year was different. It seemed like so long ago that he had met Laurie, but it really had only been a couple of months. Immediately when they had met, they hit it off. They shared almost all the same interests: country music, long walks on hot summer days, trucks, motorcycles, bicycling and more. The list of the things that drew them together was endless.

They met on a Saturday evening. Partying was not exactly how Kevin typically spent a Saturday evening but he had agreed to anyway. Shortly after he had arrived, Kevin noticed Laurie sitting in the corner. He could tell that she was not interested in the conversation. It was written on her face. She was present in the room but miles from the scene. Quietly Kevin edged his way over to the corner and struck up what turned out to be a fateful conversation.

From that moment on, time just seemed to fly by. It was as if they were meant for each other. And yet, there was that one thing. Kevin had been raised all of his life knowing that he should only date Christian girls. Up until now, it was one of life's little instructions that he had been able to live with. But with Laurie things seemed different. Kevin knew that she was not active in church, any church. He wasn't sure whether she even believed in God. Yet, despite this fact, everything seemed okay.

It was the lack of her apparent beliefs that had made him late today. Even though it seemed okay, with everything that had been going on, Kevin took time out to visit his pastor. Pastor Keith was pretty neat. Despite the collar, Pastor Keith was down to earth and always seemed to be in touch, not only with what God's people needed to hear, but also with how life really functioned!

What were the pastor's words to Kevin today?

"To love another in the highest sense of the word is to wish that person the eternal possession of God and then lead them to it."

Pastor Keith explained to Kevin that Valentine's Day was really a good day for sharing the gospel with Laurie. Our culture has embraced Valentine's Day as a day when we show those near us how much we love them. What better way than to share the Gospel. It didn't have to be elaborate or theological. All Kevin had to do was introduce Laurie to the saving grace of Jesus Christ. The most profound way to express that grace was to offer what being a child of the King meant in Kevin's own life.

B-r-r-r-n-g, B-r-r-r-ng. He rang Laurie's doorbell.

The door bell sounded so loud, Kevin's heart pounded as he waited for an answer from within.

"Hi! I've been waiting for you! You know you're late?" Laurie gently chided him as she pushed the door open and flung herself into his arms. "I love you. Will you be my Valentine?"

He had expected the question, but for some reason, he had hoped to be the first to ask. Nevertheless, his reply was quick and sure.

"Yes, but first we have to talk about something first."

"What?" Laurie queried.

"Can we go inside? I have something very important to discuss that will have a tremendous impact on our relationship."

Gently grasping her hand, Kevin led Laurie into the living room where they sat down on the sofa. "I hope this doesn't come as a surprise to you, but I am a Christian," said Kevin. "All my life this hasn't seemed to matter much with girls I have dated, but with you it's different. I truly love you Laurie, but we have a major difference between us."

There, he had raised the issue. Now he just settled back to wait for her response. And it didn't take too long.

"What do you mean? I love you too. Isn't that enough?"

"Not really," he replied. "We need to talk about what Jesus means to you, and what place He has in your life. You see, I decided long ago to follow Jesus, and to give Him complete control of my life. For me, that meant I had to recognize that I was a sinner who needed salvation, and I was willing to accept God's offer. Let me ask you a question. If you died tonight, do you feel confident that you would go to heaven?"

Laurie hesitated, "I'm not sure. I guess I believe in God. But, I am not sure what God is, much less who He is, and whether He cares about me."

Kevin began to sense this was going to be a little more complicated than he thought. He imagined that he would simply bring up the subject and somehow she would reply that she was a Christian who just didn't make her faith visible.

He wasn't sure now how to respond. "Please God; give me the words to say. You know that I love you, and that I want so very much for Laurie to love you too. Guard my words, and make her heart receptive." The prayer was as silent as it was quick, but it seemed to invigorate Kevin. He plowed forward.

"Let's assume for a moment that God does exist," Kevin began. "If you died and appeared before God, and He asked you why He should let you into heaven, how would you reply?"

"I don't know. I guess I would probably say that I have led a good life. I have always tried to do what is right. I should think that would be sufficient," she replied.

"First of all, Laurie, I love you," he declared. "You must know that. But, I have to tell you on that basis, you would never get to heaven. On the other side of the coin, I can assure you that you can know, without a doubt, that you can get to heaven! I can show you how. Are you interested?"

"Please go on."

Laurie sat back and began to listen, very attentively, as Kevin first began to outline the essentials of the Gospel message. Then he explained God's plan of salvation. As the Gospel began to unfold before her, Laurie wiped back the tears that began to gently cascade down her cheek.

"Kevin, I knew there was something different about you from the time we met. I want to have that same peace that you show in everything you do. Will you pray with me? I know that I believe, but I am not sure if I know how to pray."

Grasping her hand in his, Kevin quietly began to pray. "Lord, you alone know where Laurie has been in her life. You alone know what has brought her to this point. Please hear her prayer of confession and hear her prayers for forgiveness. Please grant her the peace that only you can provide." Kevin wanted to continue, but the lump in his throat stopped him. As he choked back the tears, Laurie picked up the prayer.

"God, this is Laurie. I understand, now, that you know who I am. Please Lord, hear my prayers. I want so much for you to enter my heart. Grant me the same assurance you have given Kevin. I am sorry for all I have done, Lord..."

As Laurie continued, Kevin began to tremble. He knew that things would never again be the same for them. More importantly, Kevin knew that things would never again be the same for Laurie. And for that, he was grateful.

Author's Insight - No Greater Love

Love. The subject seems to come up every Valentine's Day. As Christians, we teach our children that they must love everyone (even if they cannot love what everyone does). We should also teach our kids that they should not become emotionally attached to someone who is not a Christian. It is a tragedy that, all too often, we fail to give them a reason for such a prohibition.

Even more of a tragedy is the fact that we rarely equip them with the tools necessary to offer God's salvation to those in need. Short of offering our life for another, no truer love exists than the love which causes someone to lead another to Christ. There is no greater gift to offer another than the gift of God's salvation.

Many marriages falter – and ultimately fail – because people forget the love they experienced at the outset of their relationship. Married couples often wind up as strangers, waiting for an empty nest, when they hope to rekindle what they once had. All too often, instead of rekindling the fires within, couples opt to find a different kind of love.

We all know the passage that subtly instructs women to "submit to their husbands." We often mistake it for blind obedience rather than willfully giving of oneself to another. In that same way, husbands are instructed to place their wives first.

As a husband, I am called to love my wife as Christ loved the Church. How much is that? He gave everything He had – including His life – for the Church. If a man loves his wife in this fashion, she will never be wanting, because he will see that her desires are satisfied before his own needs.

The same holds true of our love for Christ. Our love often wanes. In fact, John in the Book of Revelation relates that even God asks the church at Ephesus to return to their first love for Him.

How do we recapture that love? We do so through dedication, hard work, and spiritual discipline.

At a time when the whole world is awash in the glow of romantic love during the Valentine season, perhaps we can, and should, take the time to truly explain to those dear to us what the love of God is all about.

Let's Go Fly a Kite
(March)

"He let loose the east wind from the heavens and by his power made the south wind blow." (Psalm 78:26)

Kenny could not believe his good fortune. Rarely when his Uncle Jim came to visit did they do much besides play games, talk, and eat. Not this time! When they got up this morning, and heard the wind whistling through the trees, Uncle Jim was on top of it.

"Hey, Kenny, what would you say to trying out a new kite I brought with me?"

Uncle Jim did not have to ask twice! Kenny was all over it and full of impatience as they pulled out the kites and strung them with string. Kenny's kite was just a simple diamond shape. Uncle Jim's, on the other hand, was unlike anything Kenny had ever seen. He called it a box kite, perhaps because it almost looked like a box, but it was not going to hold much with all the sides missing.

They finally made it to the school grounds. Kenny had hoped they would be first, but to his dismay, he saw that it was already getting crowded. Uncle Jim motioned him to a clear spot in the corner of the big ball diamond.

Kenny watched, with amazement, as Uncle Jim began to slowly let out the string, keeping a tight line the whole time. As he did, the kite began to soar. Kenny was convinced they were the envy of everyone there!

13

Once the box kite was in the air, Kenny tried to get his kite in the air. He struggled mightily against the wind (and apparently against all odds). He never got it more than a few feet off the ground before it took a spin, and promptly landed on the ground.

As Uncle Jim was keeping his kite aloft, he was also keeping a close eye on Kenny, watching for signs of frustration. Finally sensing the Kenny had had enough, even though it had only been about 30 minutes, Uncle Jim called to him.

"Hey, Kenny! Want to try your hand at this one?"

Kenny was aghast. What did he just say? Did Uncle Jim say he could fly it? Without a moment's hesitation, Kenny dropped his kite, right where it was, and hustled over to his uncle.

"Here. Take the reel in one hand," Uncle Jim explained, as he handed him the reel. "With your other hand hold on to the string, so you can keep it tight."

Uncle Jim let go and put the rig totally in Kenny's hands. Kenny felt a sudden burst of excitement. "Just wait until Gary hears about this," Kenny mused. Gary was his younger brother who wanted to come but stayed home, providing Kenny this rare one-on-one experience with his uncle.

As Kenny fought to keep the big box aloft (and under control), his uncle meandered over and picked up Kenny's kite. He was careful to wrap it up properly so Kenny would not have to fight with it later on.

Kenny was thoroughly enjoying himself, when suddenly a gust of wind came up that was too strong for him to handle. He struggled to keep the kite under control, as it wobbled in the air. Just as soon as he thought things were under control, and he would be able to relax, another gust hit with such force that the line tied to the kite snapped.

"N-o-o-o!" Kenny screamed. He watched with despair as the kite took off, caught in an updraft and still soaring. Kenny sank to his knees. What would his uncle do to him now?

Just as that thought raced into his mind, he heard his uncle's voice.

"My, oh, my! That was one big gust! Whatever will we do now?

We lost our kite. Hey, how about you and I go get a soda. We will have a story to tell, won't we?"

With that, his uncle began picking things up, at least the things that were left.

No scolding. No yelling. No problem. Kenny was bewildered, but he wasted no time in pitching in. After all, his uncle said something about a soda and Kenny could already taste that Faygo Root Beer on the way down.

Author's Insight – No Problem

This story is based on a true event in my life, just a few months after my second adoption happened. My aunt and uncle were infrequent visitors to our house, and when they did visit, we always focused on family oriented things. For me to get the undivided attention of my new uncle was endearing.

Yet, if there is one thing I had clearly learned about life, it was the fact that disappointments and problems will come in life. I knew disappointments first hand. I also knew that when you disappoint another, it usually comes with some sort of retribution.

That day with my uncle, I learned a very valuable lesson in life. Disappointments and problems will come, but the true test of a man (or woman) is discovered in how they deal with those disappointments. If one choses to rant and rave about how unfair life is, there is little chance to enjoy the joys that surround your circumstances.

My uncle could very easily have castigated me, but he chose to focus on the joy we had in spending time together. It was a quality time that had been devoid in my life. I relished the opportunity and grabbed it with gusto. When things went awry, I was expecting the worst but received something totally different.

The Apostle Paul was very familiar with adversity, yet he made it very clear what the attitude of Christians must be toward adversity. In Philippians 4:12, Paul writes, "I have learned the secret of being content in any and every situation." While Paul was specifically addressing the state of one's circumstances – in want or in plenty – the implication is clear. Whatever our state is, we must learn to be content.

But what does it truly mean to be content? Technically, contentment means to be satisfied with what you have, not wanting anything more (or anything else). But for the Christian, we should always want more, but not more things to have or to do. Paul is making a point in Philippians. He did not need, or want, anything else that the world had to offer. Nor should we.

Yet, we should always be seeking more spiritually! We should never be content to let life float away from us. We need to want what my uncle offered to me that day, and what God wants from us. Communion, time spent together. We should relish our time alone with God, savoring every moment and always wanting more!

When our kites go flying off, remember to savor the joy of kite flying.

Now, who wants to go fly a kite?

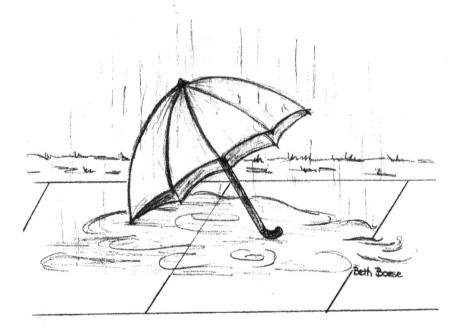

Beth Boese

Escaping the Rain
(April)

"He causes his sun to rise on the evil and the good, and sends rain on the righteous and unrighteous" (Matthew 5:45b)

Drenched, Paul shook the water off from his umbrella and folded it back into the tiny shape it had held until just a few minutes ago. The umbrella had done little to hold back the rain, and so Paul was resigned to shake the water from his hat as well before opening the door of the Steak & Ale in El Paso, Texas. He stepped into the dimly lit foyer and waited for his eyes to adjust.

"Are you dining alone this evening?" the young lady asked as she approached the solitary figure.

"Yes, I'm alone. Would it be possible to ask for a table by a window?" Paul inquired.

The young lady responded that it would and led him to a window in the far side of the restaurant, which proved to be just exactly what Paul had hoped for. The seating area was brightly lit compared to the dim foyer. Paul quickly realized, with this vantage point, he could watch the rapidly developing storm as it played out on the hot summer afternoon.

When Paul had left the offices of his client, he had emerged into bright sunshine and nary a cloud in the sky, but that changed so suddenly. Paul had little time to absorb the change. Now, he could watch, over dinner, as the storm wound its way around the southern edge of the Franklin Mountains.

Before leaving Houston for El Paso, Paul had been told that, although the city was in a desert area, rains often come unannounced and dissipate long before most even notice they had arrived. Such seemed to be the way things were developing today. As he looked around the room, he noticed that most of the patrons barely looked beyond their tables, much less to the surprising beauty unfolding outside.

The storm had appeared from nowhere. One minute the sun shone brightly, and then an instant later, the clouds began to form. Within the space of 10 minutes, the sky turned dark and foreboding. Clouds seemed perched to dump torrents of water on the unsuspecting.

Paul had every intention of getting inside before the floodgates opened, but was unsuccessful.

After ordering a New York Strip, a baked potato loaded with everything possible, and a steaming cup of hot coffee – black, no sugar or cream required, Paul settled in and watched the winds as they began to push the rain in a nearly horizontal manner. Water rose in the storm sewers, licking at the curb as if waiting for an invitation to overwhelm the nearby sidewalk.

Just as rapidly as the storm rose, the winds subsided, the rain halted, and the rising waters gave up the fight for control of the curb. Meanwhile, it was business as usual within the restaurant.

"Excuse me," Paul spoke in a hushed tone, raising his arm to summon the waitress. When she arrived, Paul asked, "Did you even notice the rain just a few minutes ago?" He truly was eager to hear her response because he found it utterly fascinating that such a storm could go unseen by so many.

"Storm? Oh, was it raining?" she replied. "It happens so often, and they last so little time, I rarely notice unless I get caught out in one."

The weather had tortured him, going from sunshine to deluge and back to sunshine in just 20 minutes, almost as if it were for him alone.

Paul finished his dinner and scribbled off a short note to the staff to enjoy the brevity of storms as they pass through life. After paying the tab by laying two crisp $20 bills on the table, Paul scooped up his receipt and started to walk away.

Then he remembered.

He walked back to the table and picked up the damp umbrella. Turning, he left the restaurant and strode confidently into the brilliant, evening sunshine.

Author's Insight – My Personal Storm

Often life has a way of creating storms that are seen only by us. While we struggle, mightily, against the rains, and are buffeted by the winds, those around are completely unaware of the turmoil encircling us. We wonder how we will ever manage to make it through. Yet before long, we are standing in the sun, stronger for having experienced the rain.

My travels in the late 1980s often led me to west Texas and the city of El Paso. I was always mesmerized by the mountains and the city that bends around them. The city has grown up in a precarious perch deep in the desert area of west Texas while straddling the border with Mexico. The result is a city that is a blend of Texas hospitality, desert motif, and a deep Mexican-American heritage. Visitors learn, quickly, that they are truly far from just about everything, except the mountains, desert, and Mexico.

The southern tip of the Franklin Mountains settle deep into the heart of El Paso, "The Pass." The very nature of the locale creates the ideal setting for split-second thunderstorms, which arise and die in a matter of moments. Yet, the terrain is such that the rains that come offer very little real relief from the desert dryness. They come unannounced and often unnoticed.

When life hits us with storms, especially during dry times in our lives, we can be sure of two things. We are likely the only ones to notice and, without proper care, any benefit derived will be short lived. We need not be concerned that no one else notices our storms. We need to enjoy everything that comes our way, even if the moments are difficult. When we learn to enjoy the storms, the sunshine is always so much brighter on the other side.

On another level, when we find ourselves in the midst of those storms, it often seems as if we are in the El Paso point, far from everything, in our lives. It seems that in such times we have to strive to get through our difficulties on our own. The reality is that we could not be further from the truth!

Something equally poignant is happening. God is at work during those moments. It is up to us to grow from them by channeling the lessons into pools of experience we can use to serve Him. The lessons we learn during our difficult moments are things that are preparing us for the future in the place where God would have us to be. Yet, He is never far from us. He is our shelter in those times of storm. When we are ready to give up is the time that we need to look up.

Bloom Where You
Are Planted
(May)

*"And Daniel remained there until the first
year of King Cyrus." (Daniel 1:21)*

Sally and Todd walked hand in hand, while Jamie crisscrossed the
street exploring. The newly formed family enjoyed the warm spring
sunshine watching the cars and people whiz by, but each pondered
life from different perspectives.

Jamie, a bright smile and curls enough for several young girls,
was barely school age and known for her constant chatter. She rarely
walked in silence, choosing instead to ponder aloud the mysteries
of life as she encountered them. The colors and spontaneity of life
that buzzed about constantly amazed her. Jamie's endless barrage of
questions simultaneously amused, enlightened, and frustrated Todd,
her stepfather of only a few short months.

Todd had a tendency to look at the big picture, searching for
the patterns of life, and was intent on capturing life as it happened.
While holding Sally's hand tightly as they walked, Todd's ever-
present camera dangled from the strap around his neck.

Sally, who had never had the joy of watching her daughter interact
so completely with a father of any sort, enjoyed their family walk,

soaking up the camaraderie, the banter, and the joy of their shared experiences.

Enjoying the rarity of silence, Todd and Sally kept a vigilant eye on Jamie, who scurried on ahead, as they ambled down the dusty street.

Although it seemed like an eternity had passed, truly, only moments had elapsed before Jamie disappeared from sight, running into the nearby bushes and shouting, "Daddy! Look! Bring your camera! Get a picture, please?" Her eyes begged the question, as if they were needed to convince Todd to snap another shutter.

Todd slipped through the underbrush, gingerly trying to replace the growth through which Jamie had so carelessly scrambled. When he reached the spot where the young girl stood, he stood in quiet disbelief. In the midst of the wild growth of weeds, grew one of the most beautiful flowers Todd had seen.

After taking several shots from different perspectives, each designed to capture the beauty of the blossom, Todd was satisfied. Jamie had already moved on and was scurrying down the lane. Sally was somewhere in limbo, halfway between where Todd lingered and where Jamie explored ahead.

Todd hustled to catch up.

Keeping up with Jamie was a constant challenge. Jamie was unfamiliar with the concept of quickness when it came to things that needed to be done. Yet, she moved with the grace and fluidity of a butterfly when flitting about outside.

Striding alongside Sally, Todd once again grasped her hand, and they resumed their warm summer walk. As they walked, Todd began to sense the importance of the moment they had just shared.

Jamie, uprooted from the only city she had ever known and thrust into a small rural community, had decided to enjoy every moment of life as it spread out before her. She had simply learned to adapt to her new surroundings and seemed to blossom more with each passing day.

Much like the beautiful flower that sprang from the patch of weeds, Jamie bloomed where she was planted.

Author's Insight – A Mental Connection

While the actual idea for this story began to foment in my conscience during a church service on Nov. 15, 2009, the story line is much older.

While living in Houston in the early 1990s and involved in a church startup, one of the couples in church were constantly beside themselves with where they lived. They had never intended to move to Houston but did so at the urging of a friend who had purchased a local refuse company. Before long, they were completely convinced they were not where God wanted them to be and made provisions to move back home. Before they left, our pastor's weekly message was titled *Bloom Where You Are Planted.*

Fast forward a few years to 2009. While attending church at Faith Evangelistic Center in Leavenworth, Bishop Keith Conard titled his sermon *Blessed by What You Do.* The message was about making our actions speak for our faith. During the course of the discourse, he reasoned that many Christians chose to pick up stakes and move on instead of learning to live where God had placed them. Conard's words still ring in my ear, "The greatest blessings are often found in experiencing God where you are, not where you want to be."

I have often spoken to others about learning to bloom where they are planted and even delivered a sermon myself on the subject many years ago. But it was not until Bishop Conard uttered those same words – You need to bloom where God has planted you – that the mental connection was made between my past, my present, and my future.

The story, as I have related it, is a true experience from the spring of 2009. While on an evening stroll, my stepdaughter wandered off into the underbrush of an overgrown yard because she caught a glimpse of a beautiful flower. She practically begged me to join her, and to snap some photos with my ever-present camera. When I joined her, the beauty of the flower, blossoming in the patch of overgrown weeds, was breathtaking.

Days later, I was out working in the yard by myself, when I noticed a flower had grown up in the sidewalk of the church across the street from where we lived. Again, I grabbed my camera and snapped a photo (or two). Despite overwhelming odds, this little blossom sprung from the soil beneath the concrete, taking whatever path available to bring forth God's intended beauty for the entire world to see. Prophetically, I likewise titled that photo *Bloom Where You Are Planted.*

The story of these two flowers and one young girl's passion for finding beauty wherever she goes, is a lesson that all Christians must take to heart. Amidst the weeds and sidewalks of this world, we are called to show forth the beauty of God's love. The only way that we are capable of doing so is if we learn to bloom where we are planted.

There may come a time in the future when God calls us to serve him in another location, another church, or another community. For some that time may come soon. For others, that day may never come at all. Either way, we have a duty and a privilege to serve God completely right where we are!

Just Call Me Dad

(June)

"Honor your father and your mother, so that you may live long in the land the Lord your God is giving you."(Exodus 20:12)

It was a very long day for Jeremy, zapping every bit of joy from his young life. But he sensed something else was about to happen, making all of today's events simply pale in comparison. Of course, at the tender age of eight, few would ever understand how he could sense such things, but that did not matter. He simply knew.

When he arose this morning, Jeremy knew this was the day they had to go to court although he did not understand why. Some lady arrived shortly after breakfast, and whisked him away. But his Dad and Mom drove separately. The lady introduced herself as Winnie. *"What a strange name,"* he thought, but kept it to himself.

Before long, they entered a building, bringing back memories he had no desire to recall. The last time he was in a courthouse, their father had taken his brothers, leaving Jeremy all alone to weep. He learned that they would be separated, forever, and Jeremy would be going elsewhere to live. When he had returned to his aunt's house to retrieve some basic things and spend a few last minutes with his brothers, their father explained that he would have taken Jeremy too, but the court said something about not being a relative. Jeremy had not heard, or understood, the rest.

Now here he was again, facing a courthouse with no understanding of why. Such a foreboding of fear wrapped Jeremy that he simply wanted to sit down and bawl. But bravely, he sucked in a deep breath and followed Winnie down the hall. She showed him some toys, which were completely strange to one unused to store-bought toys. Nonetheless, he sat down and tried to make sense out of them.

After some time had passed, Winnie came for Jeremy. Together they entered a large, darkly paneled room. Someone asked Jeremy if he would tell the truth "so help you God?" He stated, "Yes!" loud enough for everyone to hear. If Jeremy had learned one thing in his brief years, it was not to be bashful. Whenever anyone spoke to him, Jeremy always answered crisply and clearly.

Then came the questions, which were all over the place, but pretty much they were asking about his life over the last year or so. Jeremy answered as best he could. Finally, they ushered him out.

As he left, Jeremy peered back over his shoulder to where his Mom was sitting. Was that a tear worming its way down her cheek? It was the last time he would see her.

A short time later, Winnie approached him and asked, "Are you ready for your new life?"

What did she mean? No, he wanted to go home to Mom and Dad. They were not his real folks. His real father and had left him and never came back. It was the reason he had learned to hate courthouses. Apparently, now he was about to have another reason.

Sullenly, Jeremy sank down into the seat of Winnie's car and cried himself to sleep.

When Winnie woke him a short time later, he did not recognize anything.

"Where are we?" he asked.

"We are here to meet your new foster parents," Winnie replied. "Let's go see them."

Jeremy wanted to scream, "*What? Who? Why?*" Instead, he quietly slipped out of the seat and followed Winnie to the door. An older lady answered and quickly invited them in, explaining as she went that they had been waiting for them.

32

As they entered the room, a rather tall, elderly gentleman moved quickly to Jeremy's side.

"Who are you?" Jeremy asked.

"Well, you can just call me Dad..."

Author's Insight – Parenthood 101

An old expression says that anyone can be a father, but it takes a special person to be a dad. Those words have a great deal of depth, but many still miss the point. While any man can become a father, not every man who the world calls Dad is truly a dad.

The world sees a dad as someone who is there for his kids under all circumstances, regardless of whether it is a school program or an athletic contest in which their child is doing nothing more than riding the bench. A dad is the man who has a critical meeting to attend, but who still skips out, and rushing off to the obscure track meet. He gamely faces the blustery wind and rain of early April only to watch his son, or daughter, finish dead last. Most of the world sees a good dad as a man who provides for his children to the best of his ability, ensuring that they will have a better life than he.

But the Bible has a more important definition of what it means to be a Dad, which extends far beyond the world's view. First of all, according to the Bible, a Dad loves his wife "until death do they part." According to Ephesians 5:28, loving his wife means Dad loves Mom even more than he loves himself. Secondly, scripture tells us a Dad is one who is not afraid to train up a child "in the way he should go" (Proverbs 22:6). Thirdly, a Dad is one who is always there to lovingly admonish, correct, and guide each young life entrusted to him by God. Ephesians 6:4, the Apostle Paul warns fathers not to "provoke their children to wrath" but to teach them, gently and fervently, with love. Lastly, a Dad is one who is intent on ensuring that his children know the Lord. He does so by teaching them the Bible, by making sure his family attends church and Sunday School, and by teaching them to pray. A godly dad teaches his family through doing, not simply saying. He leads by example.

These things are equally true about moms. Nothing more sacred has been entrusted to our care than the life of a young child.

If you have not already guessed, I was the young lad in the story at the tender age of eight. As a youngster, I experienced the hurt as an ungodly father abandoned me. Then, an adoptive father neglected me and allowed me to be abused.

However, my life changed after that second court appearance in Plymouth, Michigan. The words, "You can just call me Dad," spoken to me by my new foster father have stayed in my head for decades. He not only told me to call him Dad, he gave me ample reason to do so. He showed me what love truly was, providing for me, being with me, and teaching me to love the Lord. Some eight months later, those same traits were inherent in my next foster home. Finally, they were equally present in my second adoptive father another seven months later.

Because of what I was taught as a child, I learned the other side of the equation as well. The Bible instructs children to "Honor your father and your mother, so that you may live long in the land the Lord your God is giving you" (Exodus 20:12).

From where I sit, I have been blessed to have known true godly dads. I have also learned that those Dads were merely showing me what our Heavenly Father is like, for God is the ultimate father figure to those who call on His name.

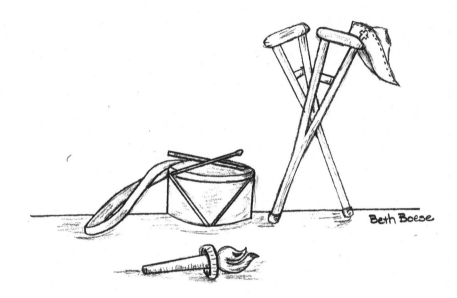

Beth Boese

One Nation Under God
(July)

"Blessed is the nation whose God is the Lord." (Psalm 33:12)

Even with the crutches, Peter felt a little unsteady on his feet. This certainly was not how they had planned to spend the Independence Day holiday. His kids had been looking forward to the community parade and barbecue in the park ever since the homeowner's association had announced the plans right before Memorial Day.

For many years, Independence Day in the community had simply been a holiday with no one home as everyone headed in different directions. Yet this year, the homeowner's association had decided that it was time to bring people together again. As it turned out, they really did not need a reason to do so. The community had suffered tremendously during the past year, having survived a direct hit by Hurricane Alicia in August of the previous summer. Even as many were still cleaning up, a terrible freeze hit in December, ruining Christmas for many and leaving widespread water damage in many homes. Then, in April, an unusual microburst tornado swept along the back of the community, wreaking havoc once again.

Each time the community had rallied, helping those who needed help and providing comfort and support. Perhaps more than anything, as an increasing number of families were choosing to try to regroup elsewhere, this celebration was intended to stem the outflow. Soon

Peter and his family would be among those relocating. Something the kids had yet to discover.

Then Peter had decided to help roof the new church. While walking along the roof, very gingerly because he was uncomfortable with heights, Peter felt a twinge in his knee. Two days later he was under the surgeon's scalpel, just days before the big shindig.

He was still unsure about how things had unfolded, but Peter's family had talked him into walking in the parade with his kids as a wounded soldier. His oldest daughter, Karen, had dreamed up the bright idea for the whole family to go patriotic. She had even insisted on creating her own Statue-of-Liberty costume. At just eight, her deep thoughts often amazed both Peter and his wife, Kate.

"Think of it," Karen had pleaded. "We live in a land where we are truly free to do anything, or to be anyone. We live in a land where people can love God and we can love those around us. Please?" To understand what freedom really meant was a profound thought for an eight-year-old, their eight-year-old. Her eyes begged him to say yes and, as usual, he conceded.

Karen's sister, Joy, had managed to latch onto someone's old nurse's uniform and was going as Peter's escort. Tad had chosen to dress as a drummer for the American Revolutionary Army. Kate had been content to soak it all in and snap as many pictures as possible.

"Daddy, are you ready yet?" Joy called from below.

"Just a minute, Pumpkin" Peter replied.

Despite the promise of one minute, Peter took the better part of five getting down the stairs and into the car. Before long, the whole family was driving down to the parade assembly area.

As they piled out of the car, folks gathered, from all over, to view their ensemble. With each gush of amazement, and hysterical cry of glee, the family seemed to draw even closer.

Marching, actually walking, as best he could on the thrift store's old wooden crutches, the motley crew made their way along the streets. Everyone they passed clapped and cheered. Soon, it was obvious they had become the darlings of the parade. In fact, it came as no surprise, when they were later chosen as the "Most Patriotic" entry.

The remainder of the afternoon became a blur. Peter simply settled into a lawn chair and tried to absorb as much of the festivities as possible, greeting everyone who stopped by. He truly enjoyed seeing his children play with their neighbors and classmates this one last time.

Finally, dusk began to settle in. One family, and then another, opted to pick up their belongings and headed off; most to try to gain a good vantage point for the fireworks in nearby Houston. It was not long before they were nearly the only people left. Peter felt a twinge of guilt knowing that in just a week they would be leaving the neighborhood and all their friends.

"Peter, I'm glad to see you're still here!" called their next-door neighbor, Ron. "We have a big van and are headed into watch the fireworks. Would you like to join us?"

Ron always had a knack for showing up at just the right time. In a matter of minutes, the whole troop was loaded into Ron's van.

"We'll come get your car later," Ron stated matter-of-factly. "Come on, let's go…"

Author's Insight – Understanding Freedom

Often we hear, "Freedom is not free." I am unsure where the phrase originated. It is an oft repeated reminder to honor our veterans and to remember those who are still fighting to ensure freedom for future generations, not only for Americans, but for peoples around the world. Our freedoms are often taken for granted, but they are just as likely to be limited by those who disagree.

Throughout the last decade, the political climate in the United States has fallen into shambles. Some citizens have begun pushing limits on our freedom of speech, our freedom of religion, our rights to bear arms, and, for many arrested, even the right to a proper trial.

Those who would have everyone repeat the same mantra in lock step fashion are trying to put a limit on our freedom of speech.

Often the right to a proper trial is threatened through muted tones in protests and through trial by media long before the facts are known.

The right to bear arms is an anathema to those who are afraid of firearms, and a bane to those who wish to control others without fear of retaliation.

But it is the right to our freedom of religion that seems to be under the most intense scrutiny these days, with shouts for Sharia Law and equality for all. Within this nation, everyone has the right to worship the same as Christians, Jews, and myriad eastern religions. That we must not bring our beliefs into the public arena has, now, become a legal battle. Somehow, the enemies of our nation's Christian roots are, gradually, erasing the memories of our national heritage.

Yet, the eternal Word of God held our nation together in those early days of formation. While some of our forefathers, who helped develop our nation's first rules for self-governance, may have been deists, the truth is the vast majority were Christians. The dominant reason that most of the colonies were formed was to ensure the freedom to worship by various Christian groups, from the Puritans of New England, to the Quakers of Pennsylvania and to the Roman Catholics of Maryland.

Unfortunately, with the eroding of our religious heritage, we are also seeing an erosion of faith in our society, a quiet dying of our churches. We must learn to stand tall, once again, and call on the name of the Lord. Only when we are once again "one nation under God" will we be able to ensure that the freedoms, paid for by the blood of patriots, will endure.

Our armed forces have sacrificed, bled, and often died, for our nation. The truest freedom of all was also paid for through the sacrifice of blood, the blood of our Lord Jesus Christ, who died on the cross of Calvary for our sins.

Let us draw near to God and fervently pray that we may again be "one nation under God."

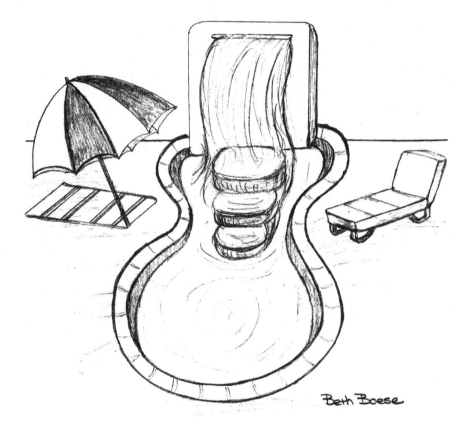

Beth Boese

A Hot Summer Night
(August)

"The burning sand will become a pool, the thirsty
ground bubbling springs." (Isaiah 35:7)

Even by Texas standards the August weather was hot and muggy, making the pool inviting, a stretch for Jim because he so seldom frequented the pool. Sure he could swim. He simply never really wanted to because he always had much more exciting things to do. Today was different from the outset. Normally very much a people person, Jim simply had sought solitude throughout the day.

This birthday had been far more stressful than he could remember for two reasons. First, he had not even received so much as a phone call of acknowledgement from anyone. Secondly, the events of the previous day had left him emotionally drained.

Saturday had been especially difficult for Jim, adding to his sullen outlook for this birthday because it dawned with service of a protective order, courtesy of the courts that would, eventually, decide his pending divorce. Jim had worked so hard to change his life and to recoup the joy they once had, but all had been in vain. His world came crashing down. While Patricia's friends and family had urged her to go her own way, little did he expect it to develop the way it had. A few frantic phone calls confirmed his worst suspicions. Jim learned the very counseling service he had been using for his recovery had been the same which encouraged Patricia to seek a protective order.

He felt betrayed, a foreboding sense that had lingered through the night and on into Sunday morning.

For years they had celebrated Sunday mornings and birthdays together as a family. Now the two fell on the same day, and coupled with the events of the previous day, Jim was very out of sorts. Consequently, he chose to attend a completely different worship service this morning, sneaking into the back row just before the service began and leaving just as the last song had started to play.

During the afternoon, he had wandered the streets of downtown Houston, which on any other day would have been bustling with people and activity. Today it was quiet, almost forgotten by those who called it home. Today, the emptiness was acceptable, almost cathartic.

When Jim finally made it back to his quaint apartment, sparsely furnished in new bachelor style, he had checked the phone. The answering machine blinked the time, repeatedly reminding him of his new status in life. Alone.

So, resolving to at least make something out of the day, Jim donned a bathing suit and opted to take in the last glimmers of sun before the evening set in. Now late in the evening, Jim sat back in the chaise lounge feeling more alone than he had in many years.

Despite the heat and humidity, Jim had been surprised to find the pool completely empty when he had arrived. It had apparently been so for some time too. There was not a single wet foot print adorning the pebbled walk.

As he looked around, Jim began to carefully observe the details in his surroundings. The pool was much different from most apartment pools he had seen. It was neither round nor square, but neither was it oval nor rectangular. Rather it was formed of a deep mosaic tile in a gigantic S-shape. At one end, a grand fountain stood sentry by the clubhouse. Water cascaded from the fountain into a shallow pool and flowed through a stepping-stone pathway into the deeper water. A rose-petal pink, pebble stone trim made the water appear much deeper than it actually was, surrounding the surreal pool.

Jim gazed in amusement at the clear, azure sky with nary a cloud in sight. The winds whispered through the stately palms. Jim easily became entranced, slipping deeper into the inner recesses of his mind, which sheltered him from reality.

The fountain's gurgling water broke into the silence, and beckoned Jim back to the scene spreading before him. Any hint of light had long since disappeared from the moonless sky, leaving nothing but the glow of the artificial light emanating from the pool.

Resolutely, Jim grabbed up his unused towel, slid his sandals back on, and headed into the night.

Author's Insight – Rock of Ages

Like many of my stories, this one is taken from real experiences, this one from the summer 1989. That year, my birthday was one that I will remember for the rest of my life, but for all the wrong reasons. Yet, it was also one that taught me a great deal about my faith.

Just as the waters of the pool appeared far deeper than they were, so do our troubles appear deeper than reality. But when we are deep into churning waters of problems that vex us, this realization offers very little comfort. During those times we must confidently trust that God has promised us that He will always be with us if we look to Him rather than the bubbling water around us.

In much the same way the powerful sturdy rock surrounded the pool on all sides, the Rock of Ages surrounds us with the steadfast love of God. During those moments, when we feel that God is so far away, it is important to recall that God did not move; we moved. And, we can return. The path back is much shorter, and easier, than the one that took us from His side.

As I recall that fountain flowing down into the pool, I am reminded of the blessings, which continue to flow from the throne of God. The old song says "There Shall Be Showers of Blessings." In my life, I do not relate as much to showers of blessings because showers cause us to run from the rain or raise our umbrellas. To me, God's blessings are like a constantly running fountain, in which we can frolic, and whose waters will feed our very soul.

Through it all, I am reminded of God's loving kindness, and His promise in Romans 8:28, "In all things God works for the good of those who love him, who have been called according to his purpose." If your circumstances are do not seem to be working for good, ask yourself whether you truly love and trust Him. If that answer is true, then ponder whether you are responding to His call on your life or, like Jonah, are you running away from where God has called you to be.

Concrete and water, rocks and pipes, electricity and filters – diverse materials all blended together to build a beautiful, refreshing pool. Our lives, God's Word, our love for Him (and His love for us), His calling (and our response) are all truths that must blend together to make God's glory shine in our lives.

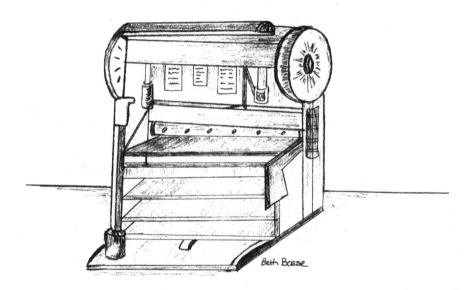

Beth Boese

A Job Well Done
(September)

"Seek ye first the Kingdom of God." (Matthew 6:33)

Ka-thump. Ka-thump. Ka-thump. The machinery continued to pound away at a steady pace. Just as steadily, John fed sheet after sheet of shiny, flexible steel into the huge press.

As he methodically toiled, John glanced about the huge pressroom. The room was big enough to put not only his house, but the houses of each of his neighbors inside with room to spare. The room was dimly lit and poorly heated, except in the summer when the heat was the biggest problem. Years of dirt and grime covered the windows that remained. Thin sheets of Plexiglas, or plywood, had long ago replaced the many windows, which had disappeared long ago. A decade, perhaps, had passed since the last vestiges of sunlight had filtered through. The floor could no longer show any visible signs of its concrete origins. It, too, was hidden underneath years of dirt and grime, with the added ingredients of many years' worth of oil and grease used to keep the machinery working.

As for the machinery, the newest press in the vast room was nearing its third decade of use. Parts were getting harder to come by. John, and his co-workers, spent more and more time waiting for the overworked maintenance staff to eke out a few more days of work from the ancient equipment. Everyone knew the day would soon come when the plant would either have to modernize or shut down.

Most of the workers had sensed an eminent closure for a long time, but miraculously, that day never seemed to arrive.

As John continued to feed his hungry monster, his thoughts wandered to what his life had become. Certainly in his youth, John had never set out to become a machinist for he had lofty expectations as a boy. He had been pretty good in school and wanted to go on to college after high school. John had wanted to become someone his own kids would be proud to call Dad. He had also wanted to be able to serve God, somehow. Now, some thirty plus years later, John was still working away at a press as nearly as old as he, and wondering what had gone wrong.

He still remembered the day he had received the call. John had just arrived at college, intent on studying accounting. His first classes had not even started when the terrible news came. His faculty advisor phoned the dorm and asked John to come to his office as soon as possible. Sensing some urgency in his advisor's voice, John rushed over. The news delivered to him was overwhelming, and set in motion a pattern in his life that would never change. John's father had suffered a stroke. The doctor's did not know if he would recover, but his mother needed him to come home as soon as possible. John knew what that meant. Being the oldest, John knew that he would have to put his dreams on hold and help take care of the family. He simply didn't have any other choice. John returned to his room, packed his meager belongings, and caught the next bus home.

John's father never did recover, and neither did John's dreams.

John quickly found work, in a local factory, as a shop-floor gopher. Gradually, he worked his way up to running the presses, beginning with the little presses, which cranked out hundreds of tiny parts every hour. From there, he gradually worked his way up to running some of the larger presses, until he reached the largest press in the entire shop. After 15 years, John knew more about the machine he ran than anyone else in the plant, perhaps even more than the engineers who designed it.

About his dreams, did he really do so badly? True, he did not become a business tycoon, but he also had never missed a day of work.

John's family never lacked for anything they really needed. Sure, they did not live in a big, fancy house. They never had the privilege of driving a new car. But, they always had shelter, transportation, and food. What more did a father really need to provide? Because of his job, John had always been around when his kids needed to talk, or when they just wanted him to watch. Throughout his children's formative years, John never missed a single school program, or athletic contest, in which any of his kids were participating.

As for doing something for God, John had always been able to share his faith and served the church in any capacity he could. He never was one for being a leader, but whenever anything needed to be done, John faithfully helped out. Whether it was mowing the grass, remodeling the garage, or repainting the sanctuary, the church had always been able to count on John's help. He taught all of his kids what it meant to love God. And, yes, how serving God, in your daily life, really looked like.

As he continued to muse, it slowly dawned on John that maybe he had done what God wanted him to do after all. He slowly began to realize that not everyone can lead and be visible. For many, the call of serving God would be a quiet life of doing the best they could, with the circumstances that surrounded them and sharing God's love to all who would listen. As the truth began to settle on him, John felt a thrill that he had not sensed for a very long time. John sensed a feeling of accomplishment.

Ka-thump. Ka-thump. Ka-thump. The machinery continued to pound away at a steady pace, shifting John back into his work with renewed vigor and determination.

Author's Insight – A Job Worth Doing

On the first Monday in September, Americans, traditionally, honor our working masses with the celebration of Labor Day on the first Monday of the month. For many hard-working people in this country that is the only labor-related honor they will receive during a typical year. Unfortunately, for most, Americans the celebration has become something less than a day to honor our workers and more of a chance to grasp one last piece of summer before it is disappears into the snows of winter.

This story arose out of my observations of the life of a friend, who had spent his entire life working at a demanding job, which he continued because it kept the bills paid and the family fed. Every September he relished the traditional, Labor Day holiday and wondered why so many had lost sight that its purpose was to honor those who worked with their hands. Often, life is difficult and unrewarding, but it need not be so. Appreciation starts with just one word of encouragement and often changes the person in remarkable ways.

An even more disheartening trend has become evident in our modern society. I do not believe it is a trend unique to Americans. We have reached a point, in our society, where we judge a person's character, and all too often, their very worth, by the type of job that they hold. This trend portends some tremendous implications, of such a nature, that I do not believe Christians can condone, much less, accept them.

The first implication is that a somehow one person's position, or rank in society, makes them better than another. There is no basis for this in scripture. In fact, just the opposite was often the case. Paul was a tentmaker (a common laborer, a homebuilder of the day), yet God used him mightily. Christ, the exalted as the Son of God, even took upon himself the form of a servant, a lowly servant, who bowed to wash the feet of his disciples on the evening prior to His crucifixion. For those unfamiliar with the custom, sandals were the common shoes of the day. As was the custom, the host provided a servant to wash off the road dust from the feet of his guests. The lowest members of the staff, the outcasts, performed this demeaning task.

A second implication is that people are somehow better because of what they can buy, or contribute to society, monetarily. This thought is troubling. It implies that a person cannot be an effective member of society unless they are capable of producing equal to others. The way I read the scriptures, no distinction is made by God in applying

His grace. Grace is offered freely and equally to all. Within the body of Christ there is neither Greek nor Jew, free nor slave, male nor female (see Galatians 3:28). If God does not make distinctions based on such matters, certainly, we do not have the right to make such distinctions either.

A third dangerous implication embedded in judging people by the type of work that they do is the implication that our jobs are, somehow, more important than our families and our faith. Even more discouraging is the implication that our work is even more important than being about God's work. This just is not so! Scripture tells us plainly to "seek ye first the kingdom of God" (see Matthew 6:33). The command is plain. It does not say, after you have dealt with the requirements of your work or when you get around to it, but to *seek first* the kingdom of God. When the Bible discusses the requirements for office holders in the church, these requirements are very specific about how one's relationship should be with the family. Nowhere does it discuss employment requirements!

I believe that it is imperative that we begin to align our priorities more in accordance with what scripture has laid out. The time has come for Christians, everywhere, to embrace the word of God, the will of God, and the work of God, preeminently in our lives. Our families must take priority over our work lives. Only when we have properly aligned our priorities can the world really begin to see the difference that God makes in our daily lives. Only when we have properly aligned our priorities can we begin to see all men as God sees them. Each is an important part of His creation, and we are equals in His sight. When we begin to recognize, and support, the reality of equality based on God's perception of humanity, then we truly can begin to live in harmony with our fellow man. Only when we recognize equality before God can we begin to change inequality based on man's perception.

How are your priorities aligned?

Beth Boese

Unmasked

(October)

"Having lost all sensitivity, they have given themselves over to sensuality so as to indulge in every kind of impurity, and they are full of greed." Ephesians 4:19

Rumors about this evening's company bash swirled around Sarah, raising her curiosity. Just about everyone who had previously attended told her, "Whatever you do, make sure you leave as soon as you can after dinner!" Although emphatic, no one had bothered to explain their reasoning. The little bit of cat, living insider her, allowed the curiosity to creep out. She was about to solve the mystery about the bash.

The company seemed to have no limit on the expenses incurred for the gala event. While many companies held Christmas parties and an occasional summer picnic, her company also threw a fall Masquerade Ball. The company wanted to build comradery and a sense of family among team members. New to the firm, Sarah had her doubts about joining in, especially when so many others had expressed their own misgivings and chosen to bypass the event.

Sarah, however, did not enjoy sitting at home. Because she was not akin to going alone, so she had prompted, cajoled, and coaxed her husband into coming. This had proven to be a difficult task since Don was not into dressing up much, especially when the occasion required more than a coat and tie. Indeed, this masquerade ball had required considerably more. When Sarah had spotted the Victorian dress and matching Gentleman's suit at the local thrift store, she knew the outfits were perfect. However, one might have thought she had asked Don to dress for his own funeral. Finally, she convinced him to dress up and go with her, reminding him that he had never met her coworkers and, most likely, they would not remember her husband.

Dinner had been superb. They had started with hors dourves, including fresh Gulf shrimp with a one-of-a-kind cocktail sauce, buffalo chicken wings, several different cheese and cracker combos, and a marvelous salsa served with flour tortilla chips. The appetizers led to a feast of prime rib and brisket accompanied by just about every kind of potato imaginable. A variety of vegetables, from broccoli to steamed carrots, all cooked to perfection, enhanced the entrees. As difficult as it might seem, the flaming cherries jubilee proved to be the coup de gras, a fitting climax to a fabulous meal.

After the staff had cleared and removed some of the tables, out of nowhere a makeshift dance floor appeared. Although many of the company offices were spacious enough under normal circumstances, but this was more room than she dreamed possible. Somehow, the quaint training room, frequently used for humdrum lectures on the company goals and methods, had been transformed into a mini grand ballroom. A quaint combo, set up in the corner, began to quiety play a mix of classic easy listening music with just a touch of country.

From out of nowhere a small bar appeared. Until now there had been no alcohol served, which had surprised Sarah. She attended too many lunches with some of her co-workers who had proven their ability to consume alcohol. Soon the bar filled, but with everyone in their costumes, she really had no idea who was who.

Sarah sidled up next to Don, and sipped on a fresh glass of iced tea.

At first, one couple, off in the corner of the makeshift dance floor, decided to take advantage of the quiet music. Then a few more couples joined in. As their numbers swelled, Sarah sensed a bit of longing to flip off her shoes, grab Don, and join in for a quiet number.

Just about that time, however, things took a turn that Sarah never quite understood. The quiet tempo changed to a louder, faster beat. What was once classical dance music transitioned into a blaring rendition of classic rock. The couples, once dancing cheek to cheek, formed a conga line and began to roam through the crowd, urging anyone, not in the action, to get on their feet and join in.

Sarah prayed hard that she and Don could blend into the wall because it simply was not her idea of a good dance tune. Thankfully, the conga line turned back to the middle of the room just before reaching her and Don.

The evening's quietness, and innocence, quickly dissipated. No more couples filled the floor. It had become a wild free-for-all reminiscent of a college frat party. She turned to Don and started to say something when she caught a glimpse of something out of the corner of her eye.

Throughout the course of the evening, it had been difficult to ascertain who was who behind each mask, but tidbits of conversation had allowed her to associate certain names behind some of the costumes. Blondie, not her real name, but the one everyone used to describe her because of her obvious dye job, was the secretary to the company president. Normally Blondie acted professional and reserved; the quintessential executive assistant who made her boss look good no matter what he did.

But Sarah caught something from corner of her eye that made her gasp in horror. What in the world was Blondie doing? Was she really about to…

No time to waste, she grabbed Don by the arm and stated matter-of-factly, "We have to go. Now!"

Without missing a beat, she pulled him from his chair and hurried to the door. She had no desire to know any more about what was going on. She really did not want to know any more about who was behind each of those masks. The less she knew, the better off she would be when Monday rolled around.

Arm-in-arm, Sarah and Don strode through the door and out into the night.

Author's Insight – Are You Real?

The Apostle Paul reminds us in Ephesians 4:17 that "...you must no longer live as the Gentiles do, in the futility of their thinking." We are set apart for God, different. Yet, the allure of the world often draws us in unknowingly at our most vulnerable points. Those points, often, occur because of situations we voluntarily choose. Such was the case in this story.

Warned not to attend, Sarah chose to go out of curiosity. With yet another admonition to leave as soon after dinner as possible, Sarah disregarded the second warning as well. Soon Sarah found herself in a place where she did not belong. Fortunately, she took advantage of an escape.

Often in life, we find ourselves in just such a quandary, but disregard all warnings and plunge straight ahead until we no longer have the sense, or desire, to escape.

Allow me to elaborate based on two different issues in my life.

I am a recovering alcoholic who has been sober since March of 1989. I should never have found myself in such dire straits. The son of an alcoholic, though I did not know it at the time, I should never have taken my first sip. There were opportunities to avoid it altogether.

My Bible-Science project in eighth grade detailed the dangers of alcohol. This project won first place in the National Association of Christian Schools National Spring Meet in Danville, Illinois. I truly knew what alcohol could do. Of all people, I knew better. I had the facts to bear it out. I chose to ignore those facts.

Due to peer pressure, I did, ultimately, partake of that first alcoholic beverage. As a freshman at Texas Lutheran College in Seguin, Texas, I found myself trying to fit in. In November, quite some time after our arrival, a group of us gathered for pizza on Friday night as our custom had become. I had continually stood firm to this point. Typically, the group would order pizza and a pitcher of beer, while I ordered soda. That fateful evening, someone actually poured me a beer and dared me to "just try one." I did. Our custom quickly became second nature. Eventually it was something we did without the pizza.

Maybe we were feeling our freedoms. We had just reached the age of adulthood where we were eligible (and required to register) for the draft. Many of us were away from home for the first time. Plus, the age for alcohol had just been lowered to 18. Whatever the reason, drinking alcohol was not – or should never have been – the right choice for me.

God promises He will not allow us to be tempted beyond what we can withstand. He will give us the fortitude to stand fast, and resist, those temptations. He has given us a choice and asks that we choose Him, but He will not force us to do so. He wants us to choose Him, and worship Him, and follow Him because of our choice. Anything less than our own desires to love and serve Him is not honoring Him.

Unfortunately, we often live one way publicly that is very different from how we live our personal lives. The differences become even more pronounced when the effects of relaxation, especially that enhanced by alcohol, kick in. We are called by God to live the same whether in public or private, a definite challenge in a fast-changing world. What was once considered acceptable, and the norm, is now often ridiculed because it is now out of touch and out of fashion. Being real to our faith becomes a bigger challenge with each passing year.

Sarah chose a way out – and a way to be real and uncompromising. Eventually, I did as well. But in both circumstances, the evil could have been avoided entirely. How about you? Are you ready (and willing) to heed the call, listen to the warnings, and serve God in all circumstances, by staying true to the call to holiness He asks of us?

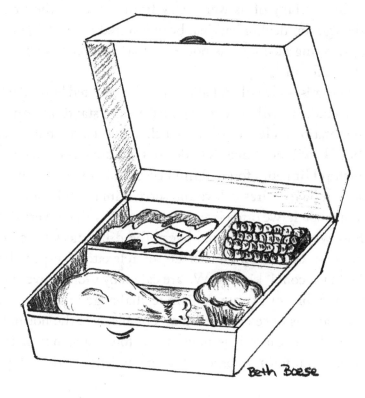

Beth Boese

A Thanksgiving Surprise
(November)

"I will praise God's name in song and glorify him with thanksgiving."(Psalm 69:30)

After finishing her chores, Amy slipped quietly into the house. She knew what was coming. Every year, it was the same old thing. Thanksgiving morning arrived and it always seemed to turn into a dismal day. The very day of thanks was anything but thankful. Dad always insisted that they go to church Thanksgiving morning. She never understood why. None of her friends went. After church, they had to go to Aunt Bessie's house. What a bore. Sure, it was all family, but no one ever got along. It always seemed that someone family member was not talking to someone else. She did not understand why they even bothered to get together anymore.

Amy was determined to make this year different. She wasn't going to go to Aunt Bessie's. She was determined to disappear before her Dad could find her and deal with the consequences later.

She quickly packed a small bag of things she knew she would need for the day: some snacks, her coat and gloves, a hat, and a book to read. Quickly stuffing the items into her backpack, she shouldered her burden and crept out the door. Cracking the door, Amy peered out.

"Oh, no!" she almost screamed. Instead, she simply murmured, "Good Morning, Dad."

"Happy Thanksgiving!" he replied cheerfully. That was Dad. Even at the worst moments, he always seemed so jovial.

"Your mother and I have been talking," her dad said. "We think we would like to try something different for Thanksgiving this year. You interested?"

"Yeah, sure," she replied, rolling her eyes back into her head. "But, what do you have in mind?"

Actually, Amy was not the least bit interested. She just wanted to get out of here and get on her way, but she knew, now, that she had no hope of escaping.

"Actually, we thought that we would go down to the Foursquare Mission and help serve Thanksgiving meals to everyone. It seems that Thanksgiving has been such a tremendously stressful time for our family that we need an alternative to our regular visit to Aunt Bessie's. Still interested?"

"Um, yeah, I guess," Amy murmured in reply. What could she say? At least it was different.

And so they went to the mission, and what a surprise lay in store for poor Amy.

One by one, the people kept coming. Amy had never seen such a wide variety of people in her life. In a little over two hours, they had probably fed hundreds of people and every one of them was different.

Families with small children arrived and were extremely grateful for the dinner that was provided. Hungry young street kids came. A number of older men, who apparently had been on the streets for a long time, came to eat. Young men and young women, obviously new to receiving charity, came. The most surprising thing that Amy had seen was the number of older ladies who came through the line.

And come they did. One after another until it seemed there was no end.

Finally, though, the line dwindled to a few stragglers.

"Honey, I think we can get ready to go now. The people who run the mission say they can handle it from here now." It was her father talking. They whole time they had been serving, she had not heard him say anything, which was not like him! Maybe the number and variety of people they had been called on to serve surprised him as well.

Amy rode on in silence during the journey home. She had been totally unprepared for what she had witnessed. As their drive continued, Amy had gradually sensed a difference in this Thanksgiving Day. She began to realize, for the first time, she felt good about helping someone. She actually had developed some sort of attachment to the people who had been served at the mission.

"Dad," she began. "I want to thank you for today."

"What?" her father replied.

"I said, thank you. I never knew how good it could feel to really help someone who needed our help. This Thanksgiving has been a complete surprise. I am surprised that we didn't end up at Aunt Bessie's. I am surprised that we went to the mission. I am surprised how good it feels. I have you and Mom to thank."

"You are welcome, Honey. It has been a long time since we really took the time to show what it means to be thankful for what we have. You know, I'm kind of surprised myself. This day has been a truly remarkable experience. Maybe we can make this a family tradition. What do you think?"

"Uh, don't push it, yet," Amy replied.

With a sigh, Amy sunk down into the seat and began to ponder what she had experienced, wondering if Dad just might have a good idea after all.

Author's Insight – Gratefully His

The idea for this story formed many years ago and was originally published in rough form in my Thanksgiving newsletter in 1997. As I reflect on things many years later, I am reminded that the message is more important now than it has been in decades.

Our nation is undergoing a time of intense economic instability. Unemployment and need reaches into corners of our society that have been virtually unscathed for nearly two generations. People who were formerly middle class are now left to ponder the basic needs for survival.

As you ponder the blessings for which you are thankful, each Thanksgiving season pause for a few moments and reflect on two things.

First, ponder the ample conveniences, food, shelter, clothing, and luxuries that America still enjoys. We enjoy instant communications, leisure time, indoor plumbing, adequate housing, warm food, and cold water. Even the homeless, among us, are better off than countless millions around the globe.

Second, I ask you to consider the things that you can truly claim as yours. God has given you everything you own. Thus, your answer to the problem of Thanksgiving should be that you have absolutely everything to be thankful for. What you have is not yours to keep, but is entrusted to you by God. As such, you are expected to invest it wisely. A prudent master would expect a reasonable return on any investment.

How is the best way to achieve a reasonable return with minimal risk? The most obvious answer is to invest what you have been given. When it comes down to the things that God has given us, many of those items are not things that we can invest in a traditional sense.

The moments of our days, the tears of our hearts, and the love of God are all gifts that can only be invested in other people. Only by investing will we experience the joy which follows. We need to actively pursue those endeavors that will have the greatest potential for return to God. And, remember, Christ has already promised that God will provide the increase!

Beth Boese

Christmas All Year
(December)

"Start children off on the way they should go, and even when they are old they will not turn from it." (Proverbs 22:6)

The youth group waited, anxious for the music to begin. They were scheduled to participate in the service this Sunday. They had been busy for several weeks working on a special project the group would unveil this morning. Miraculously, they had managed to keep the project a secret from virtually everyone but their pastor. What started out as a simply request for the youth to create a banner for the Christmas season to adorn the front of the church had taken on a life of its own.

When the project had been offered in the fall, the youth initially were hesitant to take on the challenge. As in most young churches, the number of youth was very minimal. New Beginnings Church had only been around a few years. But this past year, the congregation had marked a milestone, moving from the gymnasium of a local school into their own building located one of the main drag's prime corner lots. After the moved, every Sunday brought new faces. However, the vast majority of the new faces had been families with very young children, or newly empty nesters.

The youth group had started the fall with just three regular members, and none of them were particularly adept in art. At the time, the very idea of challenging the teens seemed like a hair-brained.

But, their leaders had stood in front of the kids, offering them all the support they needed, while simultaneously suggesting the project itself could bring in new members. Begrudgingly, one by one, the kids bought into the concept but were still clueless about how to proceed. How to come up with an idea?

Brenda was the first to mention the project to her friend Kathy over lunch at school. Kathy, a very talented artist who had dreams of her artwork becoming a career, quickly jumped onboard. She wanted to be part of the project, and asked if that was okay with everyone else. Kathy did not regularly attend any church, in part, because the church she belonged to did not have a youth group of any kind. She thought, perhaps, she could kill two birds with one stone.

Then Bill invited his friend Kenny. Bill was beginning to feel like the odd man out as the only male in the group. Kenny joined in. Soon others followed. By the end of October, they had grown from the initial three to nearly a dozen youth, all mesmerized by the task at hand.

They started with a simple Star of Bethlehem scene, a bright silver silhouette star shining over the dark background of the City of David. The group had fun working together on the scene, and it began to take shape rather quickly.

Then, someone had the bright idea that they should match the Bethlehem scene with another one telling the Easter story, which could be used in the spring. Although similar to the original scene, they chose to design a silhouette of the empty tomb using a different color scheme, with gold on purple to signify the majesty of Christ.

With still three weeks to go before Advent, and the hanging of the Christmas banner, the kids were building a bond and establishing the preeminence of Christ in their lives

Upon seeing the two finished banners, their youth director, Tom, spoke up. "You know, something is missing, something important, don't you think? I mean you've told the Christmas story and the Easter story, but what happened in between?"

To a person, they looked at Tom, in bewilderment, until Emily finally popped up, "Of course! We missed Good Friday! Well, we actually missed everything else in between too, but Easter would not be possible without Good Friday!"

A frantic couple of weeks followed, with the group quickly putting together yet another banner. For this banner, they chose to blend the colors of the other two. They started with a dark blue background and blended it into the royal purple as the banner flowed from left to right. The left side scenery was all in silver outline, while the right was in gold. In the middle, a dark black cross, bordered in gray to make it stand out, displayed the stark reminder of Calvary.

As they continued their working, the wheels of imagination spun yet again. This time, Becky had an idea. She suggested asking the church if they could hang all three banners, and leave them displayed through Easter as a constant reminder that Christmas is only the beginning.

Pastor Tom said he would see what he could do and the next week proceeded to tell them the idea been approved. The appropriate changes would be made in the sanctuary for all three to be hung on the first Sunday of Advent.

Now, here they were in the narthex, joined together as one body, set to march in and hang the banners they had worked on so meticulously.

On cue, the youth slipped quietly into the sanctuary and split into three groups. Each group hung a banner as planned and stepped back. Simultaneously, each group unfurled the banners with the pull of a draw string from each. Expectant pause gave birth to thunderous applause.

The youth turned to each other beaming, and shrugged their shoulders. No one remembered which one of them started the singing because it happened so fast. But in very little time, the congregation joined them as the chorus of Joy to the World began to echo throughout the worship center.

Author's Insight – Take
My Children Please

A church will rise or fall according to whether or not young people are active in the body is an eternal truth. Whether they be grade school age, or late teens, those with neither group present will succeed for a while, but the reality will, eventually, give way to the inevitable. Only a few congregations, who lose contact with the youth, are ever able to return from life support. How to draw in and keep young people is a question that perplexes even some of the most learned scholars.

Many churches aim for young families, hoping they stick around to form a nucleus for an eventual teen program, but such an approach takes years to develop. In the meantime, how do you deal with those few youth who come with their families, and languish because they are the sole members of a non-existent program? Others focus so completely on attracting youth, they forget the real issue is ensuring these young people grow in their faith, and are ready to live in the real world when they leave behind familiar settings.

But it does not have to be so difficult.

I am of a mind that the answer really lies somewhere in the middle. Any congregation, which includes young children, has hope for the future, provided there are enough options to keep the families around for the long haul. But those churches with only a few kids can hope for the future by making sure children are involved in the faith life of the church. They cannot be squirreled away to the dark corners of the church on Sunday night (or any other night) only to surface sporadically, or for family oriented events.

Congregations must nurture, and involve, their youth every week and in every circumstance. If kids are involved (and excited), they are more likely to speak to their friends about what is happening at church. If they talk, interest will blossom. With the blossom, eventually, comes the fruit. While the growth may only come one more kid at a time, each new life involved is another life is changed.

By convincing church leaders their project was worth doing, the kids in the church experienced success, and the entire congregation appreciated their contribution. They were noticed, they were appreciated, and excited. While adults thrive on being appreciated, young people thrive even more so.

Every church must, ardently, evaluate how they have integrated their youth into the mainstream of the congregation. If kids are involved, and the generations interact, mentoring can happen, which is where real spiritual growth begins to flourish.

The Terrible Twos

"Start children off on the way they should go, and even when they are old they will not turn from it." (Proverbs 22:6)

"I want!" Randy said, pointing to the small toy on the shelf near where he and his mother, Joy, stood. She had always enjoyed shopping with Randy, getting them out and away from the house. However, with each passing day the joy lessened; something other mothers had warned her would come.

"No," his mother replied quietly. "We're not buying any toys today."

"Me!" Randy screamed. At nearly two and a half, Randy was the poster child for the proverbial terrible twos.

"Not today," his mother quietly replied.

Undeterred by his mother's refusal and her quiet responses, Randy shrieked and began throwing his customary tantrum.

Joy, full of anything but what her name implied, let out a deep sigh, fully aware of where this was heading. Calmly she picked up the young lad from where he had planted himself in the middle of the aisle.

Randy increased his efforts to get his mother to give in, drawing the attention of anyone within earshot.

Joy left her shopping cart in the middle of the aisle and began her customary walk to the exit. She knew someone would have to take care of the items she left behind, but at this point, their exit was far more important. Imperative not to acquiesce to Randy's tantrum, she wanted to remove him as quickly as possible so as to preserve the sanity of other shoppers.

Randy continued to scream as loudly as humanly possible for a two-year-old. Plus, he had begun a full assault with all four limbs.

Reaching the car, Joy struggled to open the door, but soon had Randy seated in his car seat and closed the door. She could still hear his tantrum as she leaned against the door and prayed again for strength.

Unbeknownst to Joy, a kindly old lady had watched the events unfold as Joy had struggled with the lad. The lady approached her so quietly that Joy was startled when she spoke.

"You have the patience of Job," the lady began. "Trust me when I say this, but it will be worth the struggles." With that, the lady leaned forward and gave Joy a deep hug.

Just as quickly as she had arrived on the scene, the lady disappeared into the maze of vehicles.

Joy stood for a moment bewildered. But she felt strengthened by the angel who had affirmed her struggles.

Quietly Joy opened her door and slid into the driver's seat.

Randy had watched with deep interest the lady who had approached and then vanished. Either because of what he observed or because he knew he had lost the battle, the young child settled back into his car seat, now quiet and seemingly content.

Buckling her seatbelt, Joy started the car and shoved it into gear. While she knew that she would face the same battle again on another day, she knew she had done the right thing. She pulled from the parking space and headed for home.

Author's Insight: Parenting 101 Is Not Easy

Perhaps I have seen this more than most because of my recent two years in the hardware department at Walmart, but the situation described above is all too real. I remember very few shifts during my hardware days when I didn't hear at least one screaming child. All too often the events were not as hoped and hardly ever are they in the best interests of the child as parent after parent simply gave into to their children instead of responding to circumvent the tantrums.

When your child is throwing a tantrum, you have limited options and none are really pleasing.

The easiest alternative, and one that I saw play out most often, is that the parent caves. Regardless of their age, a child learns nothing substantive with this approach. However, a child does learn that bad behavior gets them what they want; they get their way the next time… and the next time…

Another easy alternative for many parents is to simply punish the child, right there for the entire world to see. Unfortunately, I have seen the punishment take two both physical and emotional forms. Shaming (or attempting to shame) a child into obedience seldom works and destroys a child's self-worth. Physical punishment is rarely acceptable and is frequently abusive. Often it is not done so much trying to teach a lesson, but rather it is an action done in anger, reinforcing children's temper tantrums.

Simply ignoring the crying, screaming child is another option. While it may be possible for a parent to learn to tune out their children during fits of rage, it is extremely difficult for those nearby to do so. In a similar manner, ignoring a crying child is emotionally draining for the child. In addition to not getting what they want, they suffer emotionally.

The mother of my story took the most difficult option. She simply removed the child from the scene. She did not ignore the child nor did she abuse him. Children learn that they cannot get what they want through temper tantrums while simultaneously learning that they are valued (and not ignored) by their parents.

Often the most difficult road that one must take in life is often the only appropriate avenue.

This story included another help for the beleaguered mother. A complete stranger supported Joy by offering a word of encouragement and offered a hug to a struggling mother, which confirmed to the mom that she took the right course of action.

When you walk a difficult road, it is far easier to do so knowing you have the support of others. Like the mother, you need affirmation. The complete stranger in my story both affirmed and supported the young mother by offering her support and a physical touch. One may never know how words of encourage may affect another's life. Life is too short, and too precious, to ignore the opportunities that life offers us.

Beth Boese

One Thin Dime

"Bring the full tithe into the storehouse." (Malachi 3:7–10)

Jimmy was ecstatic! With this week's allowance, he was sure would finally be to buy the WWF video game he had so desperately wanted. And today was Friday, the day his Dad usually doled out allowances to Jimmy and his two sisters.

His Dad had said no to the game for a long time, but he finally relented on the condition that Jimmy bought it with his own money. Working odd jobs and saving his allowance, he truly thought he had enough.

Painstakingly, he counted out his money once again. Yes! He had $42.25. With the dollar from his allowance, finally, he was sure he would have enough to cover the both game and the taxes.

Unsure of how much tax would be charged, he decided to ask. "Dad, can I ask you something?" Jimmy queried as he sauntered into his father's study.

"Sure, Jimmy," his Dad replied. "What's on your mind?"

"How much would the tax be on $39.95?"

"Ah. I think I know why you want to know," his Dad smirked. "Just a minute." Wayne, an inveterate technophile, dug out his smart phone, pulled up the calculator, and quickly had Jimmy's answer. "The taxes on that game would be $3.30," he stated matter-of-factly.

Jimmy did the quick math and immediately slumped into a nearby chair, obviously disheartened.

"What's wrong, Jimmy?" his father asked.

"I thought I was going to have enough to finally buy that game

I have wanted so badly," Jimmy explained. "I know I have a dollar coming for this week's allowance. If I used my whole allowance, I would be okay. But I know that I still have to give my tithe. I'm going to be one thin dime short!"

Proud that his son had remembered again the importance of giving to God what was God's, Wayne paused. "I'll tell you what," he exclaimed. "Sometimes those things go on sale. If that game is on sale this week, you still might have enough. Why don't we mosey over to Rick's Video and see?"

Still unconvinced, Jimmy agreed and they were soon on their way.

When they entered Rick's, Jimmy wasted no time getting over to the display case where the WWF game beckoned him. He was relieved to see the game was still there, but not surprised it was not on sale.

But, wait. What was next to it? A new game? NCAA Football 2013? And it was only $34.95!

A long time ago, Jimmy had already made up his mind to buy NCAA Football 2013, but thought it would take forever because he had seen it advertised at nearly $50. This was incredible! A whole $15 off?

Excitedly, Jimmy spun around to see his father was finally catching up to him. "Dad! Guess what? I have decided that I don't need to wait for the WWF game. They have NCAA Football ON SALE! Would it be okay with you if I changed my mind and got that one instead?"

Somewhat bemused by what was unfolding in front of him, Wayne let out a hearty laugh. After just a brief spell, he replied, "Sure son. After all, it is your money, and you know how I have always felt about the WWF game."

Jimmy scrambled around to find a clerk, explained what he wanted, and waited patiently for the clerk to unlock the cabinet and extract the game. He rushed to the counter, unwilling to even wait for his father, who always seemed to be two steps behind him anyway.

"That will be $37.83," the clerk stated.

Handing over $40 he had worked so hard to save was not as

difficult as he had expected. He took the change and stuffed it in his pocket. Grabbing his bag and receipt, he turned around and waited for his Dad.

Although excited, Jimmy sat unusually silent on the ride home. Rounding the last corner, Jimmy stopped and looked up at his Dad. "Dad, do you know what I am going to do with the rest of my money?"

Admittedly, Wayne had no clue and acknowledged as much to his young son when he said, "Save it?"

"No. I've been saving for a long time. But I think it's time to do something different," Jimmy started. "I know that God led us there today. You didn't really want me to get the other game, and the game that I did get was on an unbelievable sale. I would have simply spent the rest of it had my game been available."

"And?" his father interrupted.

"Well, maybe God was trying to tell me something. He wants me to honor my parents' wishes, which I wasn't really doing. By helping me save money, I think He would want me to use it for Him. You know Sister Mary?"

Sister Mary belonged to their church and had a passion for poor people. She was always asking people to contribute and always said that every little bit helps.

"Yes, I do," Wayne replied. "But what does that have to do with you?"

"Well, the Bible says that we are supposed to give God our tithes *and our offerings*. I haven't been too good at that last part, so I thought I would give the rest of the money I saved to Sister Mary."

"Hmmm..." was all Wayne could manage. Scruffing the top of Jimmy's head, Wayne simply beamed with pride.

"Yes, indeed. We are getting through," Wayne thought, walking toward the house.

Author's Insight – What's Mine Is God's

One of the most difficult commands for many Christians in our society to obey is to tithe. This is true for a lot of different reasons, but mostly because of options for our time and money that did not exist in the not so distant past. Television, cable, internet, and smartphone services are expenses that most homes now enjoy that our parents and grandparents did not worry about slipping into a shrinking budget. When you add the lure of club level sports on a young family, just to give your children an advantage, it becomes mindboggling.

If that were not enough, the cost of virtually everything else has skyrocketed. The smallest starter home, in many cities, is now pushing the underbelly of $100,000. Have you bought a new car lately? Insurance, gasoline, and maintenance all continue to rise. Groceries, clothing, and utilities eat away at the meager amounts many families can save.

When you consider the situation most families are in, who can blame them for skipping a tithe?

But the waters grow muddy when parents attempt to teach their children how to tithe. How many parents are comfortable sitting down and talking with their children about money? The task is not pleasant for most partners to discuss between themselves, much less with the kids. Such discussions run the risk of one of them asking, "Daddy (or Mommy), do you tithe?" It is a fair question that deserves an honest answer.

Making things more difficult are the messages from the church itself. Many pastors, particularly well-heeled television preachers, are preaching faith-based economic promises. If you are not doing well, maybe it is because you are not sacrificing enough. God wants to bless you, and He will, but you have to give first.

On the other hand, other churches are teaching that the whole concept of tithing is an Old Testament kind of thing. The New Testament era, in which we live, is more about giving of yourself to God's service. Gone are the days of financial accountability within the church.

The whole concept has become such a stumbling block, many congregations no longer even pass the offering plate. Instead, you might find wooden boxes on the wall for you to voluntarily remember to drop in your contributions. This way you are virtually guaranteed that you will never even hear one iota about your giving percentages from any of the church leadership.

Tithing does not have to be this hard. God made it clear to the Israelites that He expects our tithes and our offerings. Yet, God takes it one step further. Not only is He asking for your tithe and offerings, but He is expecting your tithe to come of the top, from your gross, not your net. When you bring in any earnings, He expects and deserves to be the first of which you think, not the last.

The message of love in the New Testament is a message of generosity. Do you love God enough to give Him your first fruits? Do you love others enough to go the extra mile and give of what is yours to keep?

We need to teach our children this message. Perhaps, we need to learn it ourselves. Maybe when we do, the church will fulfill its mission to truly bring people to Christ because it will be their only concern.

Beth Boese

No Place to Turn

"The King will reply, 'Truly I tell you, whatever you
did for one of the least of these brothers and sisters
of mine, you did for me.'" (Matthew 25:40)

Shivering, the young boy snuggled down into the blanket as far as he could. This was the coldest night he could remember in his young life. His sister was already asleep beside him, but he knew it would be a restless night for her too. Life had been rough for all of them since his dad lost his job.

Little by little, Jerome had watched the men come and take away their furniture. Finally, it didn't matter anymore. They had to leave their house. All they had left was this beat-up station wagon which they now called home. It was little comfort on a night like this. The young lad pretended to sleep as he heard his parents whispering in the front seat.

"I just don't know what to do anymore, honey," his father said. "All we have left is the gas in the tank." His dad tried his best, but lately he spent his days working dead-end one-day jobs. It wasn't much, but the work kept them from going hungry. Unfortunately, the jobs didn't leave any time for him to search for decent work.

Jerome's father continued, "Where can we turn? We've already tapped all of our folks for everything they can afford."

"I know," his Mom whispered. "And all of our friends seem to have forgotten we even exist."

Jerome had always loved the sound of her voice. It always had a soothing, gentle sound to it. But now he sensed something different in her voice. Her voice sounded so sad, so desperate.

"Let's try and get some sleep tonight. Tomorrow maybe we can go to the church on the corner," she murmured. "I used to know a couple of ladies from there. Something always seemed different about them."

The car fell silent. Slowly, Jerome fell into a restless sleep. The chill and the howling wind outside continually interrupted his sleep. Morning could not come soon enough for Jerome.

Slowly, the sun rose. The day seemed bright and crisp. The wind had quieted down, but the temperature was still extremely cold. As he looked out the window, Jerome sat up, surprised. Even though he had had a restless night, they had moved sometime while he was sleeping. He looked around the car. His sister was still asleep. Jerome prayed she would not remember these times when she grew up. His mother was snuggled up in the front seat. From where he sat, he couldn't tell if she was still sleeping, or not.

He looked around for his dad but did not see him. Then he heard the familiar voice.

"Thank you, Reverend. You will never know how much this means to my family and me. It has been a little rough lately."

"No problem", the pastor replied. "Like I said, we believe in acting out our faith in this church. The Robinson family lives just down the street. They'll help you out with a place to stay until you can get back on your feet. I have already spoken to Jim. He said he may not be able to use you as an advertising man, but he can provide you with steady work and give you ample time to search for a job in your field. The missus and I look forward to seeing you for dinner tomorrow evening. God bless you."

"No, God bless you, Reverend." With that, his father opened the door and slid back in behind the wheel. "I'm so glad we decided to give this church a try. It looks as if our prayers have been answered."

Was that a tear on his dad's cheek? Jerome had never seen his father cry before.

"I told you there was something different about these people," his Mom replied. "I really believe they live their faith."

With those comforting words, his mom reached up and gently

wiped the tears away from her husband's cheeks, and then from her own.

Jerome leaned back in the seat. If these people believed in a God that made them so much different from everyone else they had met, he would surely have to find out more about this God. With that thought fresh on his mind, his little sister stirred beside him.

"Mommy, are we gonna' go home soon?" she asked.

"Very soon, dear. Very soon."

He no longer heard the concern in his mother's voice. In its place was the calming, gentle tone he had always loved.

He sighed. Maybe things will be all right after all.

Author's Insight – Don't Let Your Hearts Be Cold

I wrote this story while I was living in Denver, and it was cold outside even for a typical winter evening. Having since moved to Hutchinson, the cold, and the problems associated with it, have abated some, but the basic root issues remain. Frigid temperatures are downright deadly for the homeless.

If you are brave enough, or stupid enough, to venture outside on such nights, you quickly realize the realities of temperatures below zero. You chill to the bone. Quickly! For most Americans the journey outside is soon replaced by the comfort and warmth of home. The unfortunate side of temperatures hovering lower than those found in a deep freeze is that not everyone in Denver, or most any other American city, has a place which they can call home. The homeless continue to drift in and out of local shelters, hoping to stay long enough to warm through to the innermost parts of their bodies. Then they are often gone again.

Homelessness is a problem that has plagued much of the world for many years. However, for most Americans, it was a totally foreign concept until the middle 1970s. An energy crisis left our economy in shambles and many people were driven from their jobs, and, consequently, their homes. Since that time much has been written, and even more spoken, about what can be done to solve the blight of makeshift cardboard tents cluttering our streets and highway underpasses. I do not have an answer to the problem, nor do I see an easy answer in the near future. I am not vain enough to suggest I could provide an answer when so many of our brightest minds have failed in the forty or so years since homelessness became a national concern. Instead, it is my contention, that to solve the problem, we must first deal with the root cause. That is where the rub is going to lie for many Americans.

It would be easy to suggest that for many, their homeless state has been brought on by their own actions. This may be true for some who find themselves homeless because of drug, or alcohol, abuse. I am firmly convinced that this constitutes only a small percentage of the total homeless population in our country.

It would also be convenient to suggest that the root cause of homelessness is corporate greed. Those who would propose this as the main cause suggest that corporations, in search of ever growing corporate profits, have driven many from well-paying professions which often provided the only safety net people had against disaster. These well-paying professionals have been replaced with lower paid employees thereby increasing corporate profits. Recent employment, income, and corporate profit as a percentage of total revenues, indicate a situation quite the opposite.

It would even be politically correct to suggest that our government is to blame for not providing an adequate safety valve, or enacting legislation guaranteeing life-long employment for American citizens.

The most politically conservative could even build a respectable defense of the premise that illegal immigration has caused the decline of the lifetime employment that so many Americans have always assumed was their God-given right.

It would be easy, convenient, politically correct, and conservatively defensible to assume any one of these positions. But such conjecture would also be totally wrong! The main cause of the current problem of homelessness, and the decline of the American nuclear family, must rest firmly on the shoulders of organized religion and upon Christian denominations in particular. Somewhere between the time of the early church and the mid twentieth century, the church lost sight of the work to which we have been called. American mainline Protestant churches became a meeting place which was preoccupied with social concerns while giving scant attention to the people behind the concerns. It is now time for a wake-up call. We, as a holy, catholic (worldwide), and apostolic church, must collectively return to our roots and the truths of the New Testament church.

To what must we return?

I am convinced of at least four truths which must become self-evident in all of our churches:

- First, we must be about the business of evangelism - calling a lost world home to an eternity with God.
- Second, we must realize that the future of the church rests with our children. As such, we must be about the task of adequately preparing them to live a life in accordance with God's will, no matter where that may take them.
- Third, we must reassess what it means to "love our neighbors as ourselves." We must be ready, willing, and able to make whatever sacrifices necessary to ensure we understand, and put into practice, this basic tenet of the Christian faith.
- Finally, we must be willing to place God first in all that we do and say. I say finally, but this truth must actually come before and after each of the previous three. It is the basic building block at the heart of each truth.

Only when we return, as a church, to our God can we fully expect our nation to once again become one nation under God. Only when we are truly one nation under God can we expect the ills of our society to subside. Until then, all of the money, all of the politics, and all of the rhetoric, that we throw out will only continue to bring attention to the plight of our families and the legions of homeless. All of the rhetoric, politics, and money of this nation will not, and cannot, solve the problems besetting us. Only our God can resolve the issues in America, and He will not respond without a firm, active, and confident faith on our part.

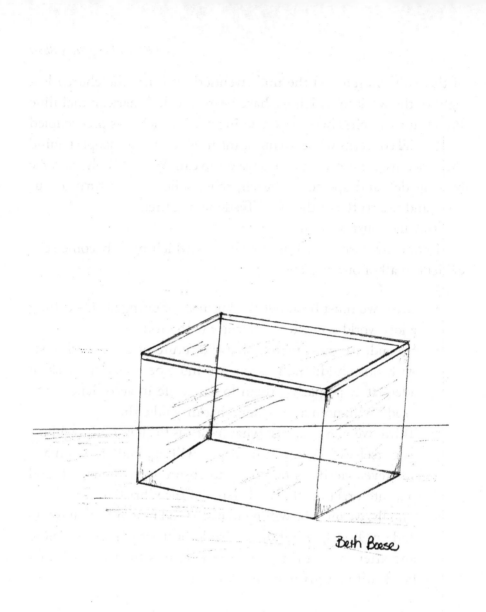

Beth Boese

The Crystal Box

"But the LORD called to the man, 'Where are you?'
He answered, 'I heard you in the garden, and I was afraid
because I was naked; so I hid.'" (Genesis 3:9-10)

Jim was in his office, filing papers, when his son, Ronnie, popped his head in the door. "What are you doing, Dad?"

"Putting away some things I want to keep," Jim replied. Normally, that would have been enough to satisfy Ronnie's curiosity and he would be off. Not this time. Ronnie sauntered in and started nosing around.

"What's the blue box for?" Ronnie asked quizzically.

"I file all of our tax stuff in that one. In the red one, I put things in that your Mom has given me that I want to remember." Jim rattled off all of the various boxes, hoping that it would satisfy Ronnie's curiosity. All of them, that is, except one.

"But, Dad, what's the clear box for?" Ronnie quizzed.

Sensing an opportunity to explain one of the best lessons of life to his son, with one quick motion, Jim slid his papers off to the side, stretched out his arms, and said, "C'mon over here, Son." Without skipping a beat, Ronnie prattled on over and returned the gesture. It had been a while since Ronnie had so willingly come to him. In recent months, Ronnie had trouble sitting still, much less climbing up on anyone's lap. Jim seized the opportunity. Jim pulled the boy on to his lap and sat quietly for a moment before speaking.

"I put everything in that box that I don't want God to know about," Jim explained.

"But, Dad... It's clear! And it's empty!" Ronnie had a habit of overstating the obvious at times.

"There's a reason for that son," Jim replied. "You see, Ronnie, as much as I might want to, there is no way that I can hide anything from God. So I chose a clear box. Even if I wrote them on dark paper, and folded them in the smallest of ways, I could never hide anything from God."

Jim sat back and thought to himself, "Oh the stories that I could tell my son..." The thoughts travelled quickly through his mind, thoughts of things Jim had done of which he was not proud. Jim knew that the day would come when much of what he had hidden from his children would see the light of day, but that time was not now. Now was the opportunity to explain to his inquiring son how difficult it was to try to hide anything from God.

"It's empty because I haven't wanted to try to hide anything from God for a very long time now," Jim finished. With that, grabbed his Bible and began to explain to Ronnie that which he had learned so painfully through the years, starting with how Adam had first thought to hide what he had done from God...

Author's Insight – Out in the Open

This has been a very difficult lesson for me to remember at various points in my life. True events in my life during the week of July 18, 2011, inspired this story. As my life began to unravel, I wanted to keep so many things secret, and I sought, desperately, to hide them even from God.

Alas, after mulling over the events of the week for quite a while, I knew I could not hide these secrets from others, for surely they would find out soon enough. I also reasoned, correctly, that if I could not hide them from other people in my life, then I certainly could not hide them from God.

As I wrestled with the secrets, the tears began to flow. In a broken spirit, I prayed out my heart to God and the story began to unfold. Many times I simply dismissed it, but then a different concept began to dawn.

Over the course of the next six months, I provided an inspirational story or poem to our congregation every Sunday morning as the call to worship. Often these were stories that were "borrowed" (with permission), but this message, at some point, affects everyone. At that point, I decided to alter my usual style of stories of 750 words or less and develop a format that was appropriate for the two minutes or so available for the call to worship.

The result is a very short story with a powerful message. I pray that it bears fruit and helps one person to realize that God knows everything we say, think, and do. There is no hiding from God.

When we confess our sins and come contritely to God, only then can we truly be free.

Beth Boese

Slowin' It Down!

*"Let everyone be subject to the governing
authorities, for there is no authority
except that which God has established." (Romans 13:1)*

The car sped along passing fence post after fence post. To Will, it seemed like hours since the last time they had stopped, but he knew it had only been around a half an hour. Somehow, for an eight year old, time always seemed so out of focus when they traveled. Will rarely paid attention to the signs as they whizzed by the window, usually, he was too engrossed in a book, or some other quiet-time activity. Today was different. He gazed out the window, glancing at every sign that zipped past.

Suddenly, Will saw a sign different from all the others. Big orange flags extended from both sides.

"Speed Limit 55." Will read the sign quickly as it flashed by and became a blur out of the rear window.

"Dad," Will began, "what does speed limit 55 mean?"

Usually Will rarely asked his father anything, because, more often than not, they resulted in long discussions about things he really did not care about. This time he threw caution to the wind, popped the question, and then sat back for his dad to begin.

"Well, it means that we are supposed to travel at fifty-five miles per hour. Normally, on the highway, we can go seventy-five until we come to a city. Then, for safety of both us and the people around, they want us to slow down because of either construction or higher traffic volume."

Will sighed and waited for his father to continue. After what seemed like forever, Will realized his dad was not going to go on and on for once. Then it dawned on him. His dad had said they were supposed to slow down, but Will realized they were not slowing down at all.

"Dad? How come you didn't slow down?"

"That's a good question, Will. I don't know."

"But don't you always tell me that I am supposed to obey all the laws?"

As soon as he had said it, Will wished he could take his question back. If he had learned anything in his eight years, it was that you didn't question what Dad did. It was always the same - "Do as I say, not as I do. I am your father and I do know what's best."

"You're right, Son. I should slow down. It's not right for me to tell you to obey rules and then ignore the laws myself. After all," his father continued as the car slowed, "God tells us in the Bible that we are supposed to obey our government as well as our parents…"

His dad soon returned to talking in the old familiar rhythm, but Will didn't listen anymore. He sank back into his seat and began to stare out of the window. With any luck, they would be home soon.

Author's Insight - Obey the Law

It seems that America has developed a national passion for speed. No matter where we have to go, we always seem to need to arrive before we have even left. Don't get me wrong. There is nothing wrong with speed. Speed is an appropriate response, even desired in some situations, for instance in a true emergency or on the race track. However, we seem to be obsessed with speed. As Christians, we need to be aware of the message that we are sending to the community around us. Actually, we need to be cognizant of several messages we send that conflict with a Christian lifestyle.

What might those messages be? I am glad you asked. (You did didn't you?)

The most obvious message that we send to the world is that we can choose to ignore any law that we don't think suits us. This kind of message presents a rather disastrous consequence. Can you imagine the anarchy that would entail if we all began to "pick and choose" what laws we wanted to obey, or ignore? Perhaps for the Christian, a more dangerous precedent is set by this type of message. If we can pick-and-choose from among man's laws, it is only a short thought away, a logical jump, to conclude we can pick-and-choose from God's laws as well. Many in our society have already chosen to follow this path of reasoning. The evidence is all around us, if we just care to look about.

A second, perhaps less obvious, message that we send to the world around us is that we think we are above the laws of men. Many who have chosen to remove themselves from the community around them. The methods of separation are many and include many groups who carry a distinct Christian message, such as the Mennonites and the Amish.

Unfortunately, many diverse sects, with passionate, irresponsible leadership, have their roots in Biblical theology but whose purpose serves another god. Such groups would include both the Branch Davidians and Waco to the Heaven's Gate cult of San Diego. They, also, have chosen to separate from society and pick and choose the laws they wish to uphold. The groups confuse people and make it increasingly difficult for many outside of the Christian community to make the necessary distinctions.

Finally, the message that we send with the most deadly consequence is the message that what God's Word is not valid for us in the twentieth century. "But," you query, "how do we send that message?" We send that message when we choose to ignore the Bible's clear command. The Bible states governments are established by God, and we have strict instructions to obey the laws prescribed by these governments. (If you want proof, take a moment to read Romans 13.)

If we choose to ignore God's Word in something as seemingly insignificant as government, or rules, with which we disagree, does it become easier to ignore other things from God's Word regarding salvation, sin and lives of purity and Godliness? Based on the number of articles written by people, including some among our clergy, suggesting other pathways to salvation apart from Jesus Christ, the leap is not one of a great magnitude. However, it is the only leap that results in a permanent consequence of eternal damnation and separation from God.

So, the next time that you feel the "need to speed," pause a moment and reflect on the message that you may be sending to your community. Consider the neighbor who knows that you are a Christian, but who has not made a commitment for Christ. If they see you speeding, reflect on the message you may be sending, and the possible logical leaps your neighbor may make based on the message received.

Beth Boese

In Perfect Order

"Dominion and awe belong to God; He establishes order in the heights of heaven" (Job 25:22)

Fred had enjoyed jigsaw puzzles ever since he was a little boy, spending hours (and sometimes days) bent over a card table and the latest puzzle. All through high school and college, despite going out for virtually every sport he could, Fred still managed to find time for his beloved puzzles.

However, somewhere along the way available time for such pursuits seemed to be in short supply. At first, the demands of a budding career ate away at his puzzle time. As time progressed even more of life's demands took him away from his puzzles.

Over the course of the past year, Fred began to reorder things in his life in order to bring stability and to ensure more time for his family. Kendra was now 13 and itching to be out of the house. Most of the time, Kendra showed little concern about whether her Dad was even around. However, eight-year-old Kaylea was much more of a Daddy's girl, constantly wanting to spend time with her Dad.

Searching for things that the two of them could do together that would not destroy the family budget was a constant challenge. They had already visited every free event, show, zoo and park that the city had to offer - some of them many times over - when Fred's wife, Shelley, remembered his affinity with jigsaw puzzles and suggested they test the waters with a simple puzzle.

Corner pieces and edges fit easily. Internal pieces were a completely different issue. Kaylea simply could not understand how some pieces fit perfectly, yet did not belong in certain spots. Separating them by color and trying to work on bits at a time seemed to make little difference.

"But, Daddy," she pleaded, "it fits! Why can't it go there?"

"Honey, the colors don't match. If we left it there, when we are done our picture will not look like the one on the box." Fred patiently explained repeatedly.

With each passing day, they puzzle had gradually taken shape and Kaylea began to bask in the glow of the work they were accomplishing.

Slowly the ideas began to sink in but by that time, the first easy puzzle, just 500 pieces, had taken over a week to complete.

"Look, Mommy!" Kaylea shouted one evening. "The puzzle's all done! Doesn't it look pretty?"

Shelley had to agree, it was beautiful. The results were a beautiful picture of one of the cutest kittens she had ever seen - far more beautiful than the illustration on the cover of the box.

Soon Fred and Kaylea were off in search of another puzzle, and then another. With each puzzle, the difficulty increased, and the pictures intensified.

Each puzzle also saw a growing interest by Kaylea to make sure the puzzle was done in proper order. She had learned that the order made the process simpler, because it made seeing the big picture easier.

Author's Insight – A Puzzler's Delight

As a child, one of my fondest memories was watching my Grandpa put together his many puzzles. He always took such a delight in doing so. Alas, all of his hard work was for naught as the puzzles are now long gone. No doubt I got my love for jigsaw puzzles from my Grandpa, but also, I have always loved the challenge of a good puzzle.

When I grew older, those memories came back as I stepped into Curtis Café in downtown Stafford, Kansas. The walls were alive with hundreds of jigsaw puzzles, painstakingly put together, and mounted on the wall.

Unfortunately, the Curtis Café closed in December of 2012, but thanks to the marvels of the Internet, the memories still live on. Feel free to check it out, simply Google the restaurant's name. You will most likely find an entry on the Kansas Travel web site.

Adding to the intrigue, I eventually met Rev. Billy Hughes, an elderly gentleman, when he was still pastor of the United Methodist Church in Iuka, Kansas, which is just a stone's throw south of Stafford. Stopping by his home one day, I discovered him hard at work on a jigsaw puzzle with one of his grandchildren. They had just completed the puzzle and were gluing it to a permanent backing.

Even with all the connections to puzzles and puzzlers, the idea for this story did not take shape until 2007, nearly two years after I had moved from the Stafford County area. In our men's Bible study group on Wednesday nights, we were working our way through the New Testament when we came across I Corinthians 14, which focuses on the gifts of the Spirit, particularly the gift of tongues.

Coming from a different background and perspective from many of the men in our group, I approached the discussion of the gift of tongues with caution. During this discussion, I was struck, not by the speaking in tongues Paul encourages, but by the admonition that he offers at the end of the chapter.

Paul sums up the use of the gifts of the Spirit, including prophecy and tongues, with the admonition the "everything should be done in a fitting and orderly manner."

All too often, in our worship experiences, the emotion of the moment can cause us to lose sight of the fact that our God is a God of order. Not of chaos.

God loves our joyful praise. Just look at the myriad examples of David's rejoicing. Yet, God also loves order. Examine closely the intricate patterns and order He created in the universe!

Not only does God expect order in our worship, but God also expects order in our lives. God has a purpose for us. With no order, we are like Kaylea trying to see the anticipated result of the puzzle. We cannot see the big picture because of the chaos.

Let order reign in your life!

Beth Boese

A Plain Brown Wrapper

"Man looks at the outward appearance,
but the Lord looks at the heart." (I Samuel 16:7)

Jenna had waited impatiently for her 18th birthday party. For many things, it meant she would finally be considered an adult. Everyone was here and excitedly milling about and enjoying the festivities. Everyone, that is, except one person. Her Dad.

She decided to give it just a few more minutes before opening her presents, just in case he was simply running late. Just as the thought crossed her mind, the doorbell rang. She ran to answer it, and her heart skipped a beat when she saw her dad had finally made it. Then her heart dropped just as quickly, when he handed her a present.

While everyone else had brought beautifully wrapped presents, some of significant size, his was puny and just a plain brown wrapper.

"Thank you, Daddy!" she managed to murmur, tossing the gift to the edge of the gift table, where it promptly fell to the floor

While opening her gifts, she squealed with delight, time after time, never once noticing the package lying against the wall.

Long after everyone had left, Jenna and her Mom were cleaning up. "What did your Dad give you?" Mom asked inquisitively.

Honestly, she couldn't remember and wasn't exactly eager to find out. Finally, it dawned on her that she had not opened his gift. She hurriedly searched, finally spotting the present where she had tossed it. Before he departed, her father never even mentioned that she had not opened his gift.

Jenna picked up the box, sat down on a chair, and carefully unwrapped the brown paper. On the back side, he had scribbled a note. "To my dearest angel, you're all grown up now. I hope that this will help keep you safe on your journey through life. Love, Dad."

Anxious now, she carefully lifted the lid of the tiny box. Inside nestled a single set of two keys, with another note. "Look by the curb in front of the Johnson's house."

What had appeared to be the most unwanted, afterthought of a present was the most needed, and valuable, gift she had received all night.

And to think she simply tossed it aside, unopened, simply because it came in a plain brown wrapper.

Author's Insight – Plainly Stated

The inspiration for this story was a real life experience one of my Internet friends experienced. Someone sent her a very unkind note, simply dismissing her, because of the way she looked. He did not take the time to know her, understand her circumstances, or her varied medical problems.

By dismissing her so matter-of-factly on mere appearances, he lost out on learning of the kind, caring, compassionate side of her that others knew. Likewise, he will never know of the good she does for other people, or the way that she simply brightens people's lives just through her simple, selfless actions.

How often do we not fall prey to the same sentiments, or experience the same disgrace, simply because of first appearances?

As Christians, God calls us to a higher standard where we view people as God sees them. We are called to look at the heart and not the outward appearance. God values every person. Certainly, we should value them as well!

When we take a leap of faith to accept people by God's standards, our lives will change forever. We will experience relationships from a whole new perspective. We may gain friendships with people we would not have associated with in our past.

Don't simply discard the people in plain brown wrappers!

Free At Last

*"Then you will know the truth, and the
truth will set you free." (John 8:32)*

Jesse had been trying, for days, to enjoy his freedom but had been
unable to do so. The reason he had been in jail did not matter. It truly
was a case of being with the wrong crowd, in the wrong place, at the
wrong time. It had taken hours for the public defender to straighten
it all out, and it proved to be an incident he never wanted to repeat.
While waiting behind bars, he had promised himself when the jail
doors opened, he would never wind up there again.

In order to keep that vow, Jesse quickly learned that a complete
change of lifestyle was in order. None of the same friends. None of
the same haunts. He swore off all of his old habits.

Saturday nights used to mean partying with friends, but not
anymore! In his efforts to change, he found himself meandering
down the streets of Grand Rapids with no purpose in mind and
no idea where he was headed. He ambled aimlessly along the wide
expanse of Division Avenue.

One thing he had learned in jail, freedom was worth everything
it took. Of all people, Jesse should have known that. He had learned
to enjoy the sweet taste of freedom the previous summer when he
left home the last time.

As a teenager, Jesse lived an absolute nightmare, full of abuse and violence. Such was life with an alcoholic father. When he left home, the release he experienced had been unlike anything Jesse had ever experienced. Relief ushered in sheer exhilaration!

He longed for that same exhilaration since his release, but it proved to be elusive. As he wandered, constant reminders of his choices lurked behind every corner. Jesse roamed aimlessly, bored, confused, and lonely.

Subtly, music began to enter the outer reaches of his consciousness, quietly at first. But it grew louder with each passing minute. The music was reminiscent of the music he remembered his Momma enjoying, but which he had long since forgotten. The music beckoned to him and before he realized it, Jesse stood in front of the open doors of the run-down chapel, soaking in the melodies, and the memories, of his Mom. The music ended far too soon. Nonetheless the chapel beckoned Jesse to come in. Quietly, he slipped, inconspicuously, into a back seat of the non-descript room.

The preacher was an unassuming man with a booming voice, a combination that quickly quieted the unease that had crept into Jesse's psyche. Much of what the preacher said simply went in, rolled around in his head and just as quickly disappeared. Then he said it.

"Do you long to be free, totally free, of your past? Are you searching for freedom that you have been unable to find?"

Jesse leaned forwarded, now catching every word the pastor spoke. ".. Jesus is the answer, the only source of true peace and freedom. Have you reached a point in your life where you have nowhere to turn but to turn around? Do you want to be rid of the ghosts from your past?"

"Could it truly be that simple?" Jesse muttered to no one in particular. The fiery preacher continued, with Jesse caught between his own dark thoughts and the promise of freedom the preacher offered.

As the altar call began, Jesse hesitated. Every fiber in his being wanted to go forward, but his body refused to budge.

With every ounce of strength he could muster, Jesse slipped from the back and began the long walk to the altar. Completely and utterly consumed, tears began to flow long before he reached the front.

"I want that freedom," Jesse prayed, collapsing before the altar.

Author's Insight – Free Indeed

The idea for this story struck me while sitting in church on Palm Sunday, 2009. The sermon was based on Barabbas, whom Pilot offered in exchange for Christ. Considering the crimes for which Barabbas was charged with, freedom must have seemed like an unbelievable possibility.

As I sat pondering the fate of Barabbas, a different thought struck me. What should have been so amazing was not the freedom offered to Barabbas, but rather Christ's sacrifice, looming on the horizon, which would offer amazing, ultimate freedom to all humanity who would choose to believe in Him.

From the time we are little children, we long for freedom even as we eagerly await the end of the school year and the freedom that summer brings. As teenagers, we look forward to the freedom that comes with getting our driver's license. Next we long for the freedom that comes on the day we move away from home. As parents, many anticipate the freedom of the empty nest. Growing older (sometimes gracefully), we look forward to the freedom of retirement and no longer punching a time clock.

As Americans, we enjoy freedoms about which much of the rest of the world can only dream. We are free to come and go, to worship God as we see fit, and to speak our peace without fear of recrimination. Unfortunately, in reality, often we simultaneously relish and take for granted our freedoms. We enjoy those freedoms, but do nothing to preserve, or secure, those freedoms.

The life of an immigrant is not an easy life. They often work long hours, with little pay, hoping to save something to send home and bring their family with them. They desire to grasp a piece of the American dream and experience freedom. I have never been an immigrant, but working with the Hispanic immigrants in Denver in the mid-90s, I learned that often the difference between those who make it here and those who return home is the desire to experience the true freedoms that America offers.

The freedom offered to Barabbas by the occupying Roman

government was a temporal freedom. Coincidentally, Barabbas had struggled long and hard to overthrow the Roman government that now offered his freedom. Surely Barabbas must have considered the possibility that the freedom offered by Pilate was only temporary.

Yet, there is no freedom in the world that can begin to match the freedom offered by God through the death, resurrection, and ascension of His Son, Jesus of Nazareth. The freedom that God offers releases us from the tyranny of our sins and the reminders of our past.

But that is not where the freedom ends!

Immigrants continue to arrive on our nation's doorstep escaping a litany of evils that include poverty, war, death, and disease; but they are also seeking to experience the freedom that comes with the promise of a new beginning. Likewise, the freedom offered by God comes with a promise of a new beginning. His freedom is not temporal; it is a new beginning with nothing between us and His throne leading to eternal life.

Alas, most Christians are like most Americans, simultaneously expecting our freedom to endure forever, but unwilling to do anything to ensure that freedom for others.

As Christians, we are called to action.

- We are charged to make disciples, which means constantly sharing the Gospel with others (Matthew 28:19-20).
- We are called to love one another, not in the sense of brotherly love but with love described by the Greeks as agape love, following Christ's example, even to the point of giving our lives if necessary (I Corinthians 13).
- We are called to obedience. The Ten Commandments are not just an ancient example for us to live by, but a living breathing set of commands to use in shaping our behavior (Exodus 20).

Only we when we live out our faith, do we truly experience the eternal freedom of God.

The Fire

"If any man builds on this foundation using gold, silver, costly stones, wood, hay or straw, his work will be shown for what it is, because the Day will bring it to light. It will be revealed with fire, and the fire will test the quality of each man's work." (I Corinthians 3:12-13)

Andy looked around the water. It just did not seem the same anymore. Actually, ever since that day last summer, nothing had been the same. Ah, yes, that day! Andy had tried to forget, but he just couldn't. He remembered that day all too well.

It had been an invigorating day, an experience that any angler would want to remember forever. Andy spent the day fly-fishing with his buddies in the clear, crisp waters of Georgetown Creek. Not one other soul was around for miles. He experienced nothing but the water, his friends, and the fish.

Andy had never been an avid fisherman, but he often went along. It was a great escape from the house, his kids and his wife; as well as a great chance to bond with his pals.

That day had been different from all the others he had spent fishing with his buddies. Andy actually caught something! He actually caught two somethings; both of them were large, trophy-sized rainbow trout.

Knowing he would never get his wife to go along with spending the money to mount two fish, Andy and his buddies debated for quite a while about what to do with them. Eventually, they decided Andy would keep one, and try to get his wife to agree to get it mounted. The other trout ended up providing enough filets to yield dinner for them all. Well, maybe not dinner by itself, but the potatoes in the fire went a long way to making sure that no one went hungry that night.

After dinner, in what seemed like a throwback to the earlier days of childhood summer camp experiences, Andy and his friends sat around the campfire singing. They sang every song they knew. When they were finished, they started them all over again.

Finally, in the wee hours of the morning, the guys decided they should get some sleep. After all, their families were due in the morning. It was never a good idea to spend a day in the woods with the kids while they were fighting sleepiness as the kids had a knack for not slowing down much.

After a brief debate over the merits of leaving the fire burning, or putting it out, they pretty much agreed that it couldn't do much harm to leave it burning. The flames had all died down. They had built the fire in a properly constructed fire pit. The smoke would keep the mosquitoes away for a while.

What could possibly go wrong?

Tim was the first to notice. He slowly wakened to the crackle of nearby sparks and the scent of heavy smoke hanging in the air. He bounded to his feet and quickly raced to awaken all of the others. Running from tent to tent, Tim first woke Phil and then Peter. By the time he got to Andy's tent, which was a good deal away from the others, they all realized that it was too late to do much of anything but run.

Grabbing very little, except clothes to wear, the guys all jumped into the beat-up old van they took camping. Bouncing down the hills winding, back country road, they raced for safety. Peter grabbed his cell phone and called for help.

Eventually, they reached the edge of a nearby town. As the van slowed to a crawl, the highway became alive with a swarm of firefighters racing out of town. The fire was quickly expanding. A ferocious battle ensued with the raging fire.

Three days and two thousand acres later, the fire gave up the fight. The fire lapped at the breeze for one final time before succumbing to the onslaught of slurries and fire breaks the exhausted firefighters had furiously built. Not one injury resulted. No homes were lost. Slowly life returned to normal for the town which had been so severely threatened and for the men who unknowingly had caused the alarm.

Several months later, as the guys were sitting around the barbecue in Andy's backyard, Peter saw it. A small article, hidden in a corner of a back section of the newspaper, revealed that the authorities had finally determined the cause of, what was referred to, as the "Georgetown fire." A small, secluded campsite had been located and determined to be the source of the fire.

The authorities were looking for whoever had been camping at that site. The article went on to explain that the authorities had no intention of bringing charges. Apparently, the campers had done everything right.

The local forest service office just wanted to talk to the guys to see if they could determine what actually happened and anything they could do to prevent a repeat of such a calamity. To aid the search, the paper gave a detailed account of the campsite.

Located just feet from the Georgetown Creek, the site appeared to have had several tents pitched in close proximity to each other, except one tent that had been pitched some distance away. The campers had taken care to dig a proper fire pit and line it with stones from the river.

As they finished reading the article, reality hit the men. They glanced from one to another. The paper described their campsite in detail. Since the fire, each of them had wrestled the question of how the fire could have started from a few glowing embers in the pit. Perhaps they would never know the answer, but the friends knew they had to come forward. They had to try to do something to restore the natural setting that had been destroyed because of their fun.

This reason brought Andy back to his favorite fishing spot.

In their resolve to do something constructive about the events of that ominous day, the group had stepped forward. In minute detail, they had described the events of the day and evening to the authorities. To a man, the stories had matched. How could they not? The events of that day had not moved very far from the forefront of their thoughts. They had volunteered to do whatever they could to help.

Quietly, Andy laid the small spade alongside the fresh hole and picked up another young tree. Slipping the tree into the fresh hole and quickly replacing the pile of dirt, Andy stared at the vast, barren expanse. In silence, he took comfort in the thought that they had only a couple hundred more trees to plant.

Author's Insight - Tried By Fire

"Pass It On," the popular Christian song of the early 1970s, started with the words "It only takes a spark to get a fire going." Fire. Very few words by themselves carry as much impact as this single word. People insure against it. Both people and animals panic at the sight of it.

Without a doubt, fire is a very destructive force. Millions of acres of forest are laid bare every year by fire. Fire kills or maims hundreds of people each year. Thousands are left homeless. When used inappropriately by our industries, fires emit tons of toxic chemicals into our environment every year.

Yet, for all the bad press it carries, few things can do as much good as fire. Without much thought, an expansive list of good might include the following characteristics. Without fire, and its warmth, most of the world's population would freeze. Many people take its warmth for granted. Fire protects us from disease carried in our food. We prevent disease by pasteurization and cooking. Without fire we would have no cars, few buildings, and no glassware. In fact, without fire, we would do without many of the things that were once considered luxuries but are now considered necessities for Americans.

Why? Fire is the medium used to turn iron into steel, clay into brick, and silicate into glass. Gasoline utilizes fire to power our cars, create electricity, and even incinerate our most toxic wastes.

Fire, one of the most powerful forces known to man, is also used by God to further His work!

In the Old Testament, we first run across God's use of fire in Genesis 3:20. After the fall of man, God used a flaming sword to protect the Garden of Eden, keeping man from returning. God once again used fire, accompanied by brimstone, to destroy Sodom and Gomorrah in Genesis 19. In the book of Amos, we read the punishment of the nations will be destruction by fire. Matthew 13:41-42 states the punishment those who choose to ignore God's call to repentance will be eternity in a lake of fire.

But, God also uses fire for good. In Exodus (chapters 3-4), God used a burning bush to commission Moses. On a fiery chariot, Elijah entered the open gates of heaven (II Kings 2:1-12). God also used fire to announce the coming of the Holy Spirit at Pentecost (Acts 2).

Even now, in the late twenty-first century, God continues to use fire to strengthen and shape the spiritual well-being of his children. Figuratively, God uses fire to try His children when he allows trials and difficulties to enter our lives. Trial by fire gets our attention, strengthens us, or purges evil from our lives. Literally, God uses the calamity of natural fire in our lives, and loss of our possessions through fire to force us to reflect on His power and glory. Such calamities can remove stumbling blocks from our lives, allowing us, no, sometimes forcing us, to depend on Him.

The next time that you feel you are being "tried by fire," ask yourself if God is trying to get your attention, to destroy evil from your life, or to remove a stumbling block that prevents you from dependences on Him. Do you need God's fire to force you to depend on Him and reflect on His power and glory? Truly ask, is God using the fire for your good?

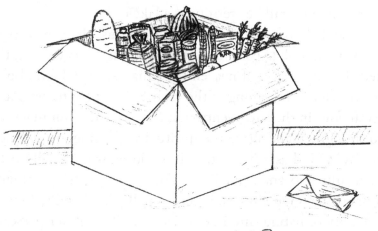

Beth Boese

The Furlough

"Look at the birds of the air; they do not sow or reap or store away in barns, and yet your heavenly Father feeds them. Are you not much more valuable than they?" (Matthew 6:26)

Ralph sat motionless before the window, staring blankly as the rain beat steady on the ground outside. He was oblivious to what he was seeing. Too deep in thought really to care about the weather, he recoiled at the experiences of a mind-numbing week. The reality of a series of difficult weeks had gradually taken a toll, bringing him to this point.

Unshaven, rumpled hair, and clad in a pair of well-worn jeans and a ratty Royals tee, Ralph was the epitome of a man overtaken by depression. He had neither the energy nor the desire to do much any longer.

"Ralph, are you okay?" Mary asked as she entered the room. She already knew the answer. Mary's concern for her husband had increased with each passing day.

Ralph never moved, failing to even so much as acknowledge her presence. Mary sidled alongside his chair and gently stroked his graying hair.

Mary knew that things had been rough for them, especially since the furlough at the plant. The layoff had been extremely difficult for Ralph to take. He had been employed with the company for nearly two decades, working tirelessly whenever he was asked. He had been the quintessential company man, but that meant little when the economy soured.

Ralph had aged gracefully through the years with the slight gray streaks, intruding at the edges of his hairline, the only hint that he was nearing 50. In every other way, Ralph looked like a man much younger. He was muscular, square-jawed, and ruggedly handsome.

However, companies did not hire on how one looked, but on what a person knew and what someone could offer. With only a high school diploma and very few computer skills, Ralph was a man from another time.

As the weeks had slipped by, Ralph always feared this day was coming. The last unemployment check arrived in the mail just this morning. Once it was spent, few options remained. Certainly, no options existed that he had been able to find.

Slowly Ralph mentally returned from wherever his mind had ventured. Turning to look at his wife, the beleaguered figure softly replied to her question, "I simply don't know, Mary." Truly, he didn't.

Mary fully understood Ralph's reply, but her faith had continued to be strong despite the difficult circumstances. "Ralph," she whispered as she knelt in front of him and placed her hands in his. "We can get through this. I don't know how either, but I know God will provide. We simply have to keep faith." She believed those words with every ounce of her being.

Ralph gazed into his wife's eyes, the deep, penetrating eyes that had so passionately drawn him to her so many years before, and replied, "I know. I just wish that God would provide us a sign that He knows our plight and He desires to see us through."

Lost in their brief exchange both failed to see a car pull into the driveway. The doorbell chimed, which startled them both. As Mary rose to answer the door, Ralph glanced out the window just in time to see the car pull away as silently as it had arrived.

Unaware that their visitors had left as quickly as they came, when she opened the door Mary was surprised to see no one was in sight. She almost missed it, but as she turned to close the door, Mary caught a glimpse of the box filled with groceries that the visitors had left on the stoop.

She threw open the door, picked up the box, and turned to go back inside. As she did, a gust of wind swirled and caught an innocuous envelope, tucked in with the groceries, sending it flying into the foyer.

Rising to help, Ralph walked purposefully to the door, stooped down, and retrieved the missile. Opening the flap, he slid out the enclosed card out. As he opened it, a crisp one hundred dollar bill fell to the floor. Ralph read the card, "Remember the angels who walk among us."

He sank to the floor. Tears began to well up, but Ralph fought them back. He silently began to pray, thanking God for remembering his family in their hour of need. The shroud of despair that had taken hold of his life lifted slightly. Suddenly, a glimmer of hope sparkled.

Author's Insight: A Matter of Faith

This story is loosely based on an incident that happened to me some 30 years ago, but I was off work due to an auto accident rather than a souring economy. Because it was an auto accident, unemployment was not available. I had traded cars the weekend before my accident, but was uninsured because of a quirk in Michigan's auto insurance laws. I had no coverage for my auto, my health, or my loss of income. Some six to eight weeks later, we had no groceries in our home, very little fuel in the LPG tank that heated our mobile home, and mounting bills to pay. One day after visiting with some friends, we returned to find two bags of groceries and a $100 bill neatly tucked in an envelope in one of the bags. To this day, I do not know who the benefactor was, but I remain convinced that it was indeed an act of angels among us.

As many people continue to struggle with unemployment (and underemployment), keeping one's eyes on God as the source sustaining us is increasingly difficult. Christians are not exempt from the depression that roots in difficult circumstances. We must constantly remind those who are so affected that God will provide for those whom He has called and who love Him.

But the message must not end there. In difficult economies, each of us might be called up by God to carry out acts unfamiliar to us. While we are not angels, we might be called upon by God to serve in that capacity to people who are in need. If we truly follow the example of Christ to love others as He has loved us, we will be attentive to the needs of others, especially fellow Christians. When we see needs that people have no way of meeting, we must be ready and willing to help. Giving *under the cover of darkness* will draw (and keep) the attention and glory toward God, not on ourselves.

It can be no other way.

Beth Boese

A Knock at the Door

"Here I am! I stand at the door and knock. If
anyone hears my voice and opens the door,
I will come in and eat with that person, and
they with me" – Revelation 3:20

Answering the rap on the door, Peter was surprised to see the young man standing there. Perhaps the word teenager would more aptly describe his age, but nothing else about him indicated he had any business being here.

Peter ran a youth home. Most of the kids came from pretty much the same background. Very few of the kids really had any problems, most came because of one special person. Their common benefactor thought that they deserved more out of life than what they were experiencing. Most had come to know their benefactor, Peter, shortly after arriving, but many remained in the dark for as long as they remained.

The youth standing at Peter's door now was vastly different from any who had previously darkened his doorway. "May I help you?" Peter queried.

"I don't know who sent me here, but I was told to tell you that I have been chosen by Jawan," the young man stated. "He said that he has sent many kids to you and you have always taken them in," he continued. "The man who sent me also said you would be able to show me what I needed." After stating his purpose, the teen just stood peering through the doorway, not knowing what to do or what to expect.

Unfortunately, at this point, Peter was also unsure of what to do. What the lad had said was true. Peter infrequently turned anyone away. The young men sent by Jawan were never sent away. Occasionally some who had come seeking answers, or a better life, left when they found out how difficult things could be, but those left by their own choice.

All of the previous "door knockers" had come from the same general background. They shared an identity apart from their calling by Jawan. They shared ethnic, social and economic background. These youths shared a culture to which this young man obviously did not belong.

Peter stepped back and opened the door. "You might as well come in," he stated flatly. Inwardly Peter cringed. Peter knew this day was coming. The community around them had changed so much through the years. Turning his attention back to the matter at hand, Peter called out.

"Hey, you guys, come here! I want you to meet someone." As soon as he had spoken, Peter realized he didn't even know the name of this young man.

"I am sorry for being so rude, but I'm Peter. I didn't catch your name. You are…?"

"Rasheed," the boy replied quickly.

Suddenly, they were awash in a sea of teenagers wondering what the commotion was all about. Immediately they surrounded Rasheed, making him feel welcome. Not one of the guys, not even for a moment, questioned why Rasheed was there. Somehow they all sensed he had been sent to join them. They assumed, quite correctly, that Rasheed was just one more of the chosen who were expected to mature together, becoming a family.

Peter stepped aside and let them take control. Soon enough Peter would begin his task of teaching the newest member of the household. For now the assimilation process was more important, and going better than Peter could have imagined that it would.

Perhaps Jawan knew what he was doing after all.

Author's Insight: They Are All My Children

The inner city church is dying. Dr. Richard J. Krejcir (2007) cites US Census Data in concluding that every week an average of 76.9 churches close while on average a mere 19 new churches open. Most of the new churches will open their doors in predominately white, suburban enclaves. Melissa Steffan (2013) offers that what once was the most dominate nation sending missionaries abroad has now become the largest receiving nation of missionaries, receiving nearly 32,400 missionaries from other lands in 2010. Indeed, the church as we know it is in danger of becoming extinct!

I grew up in a denomination noted for its Dutch roots. Among longtime members, it was common to hear someone utter the statement, usually in jest, "If you ain't Dutch, you ain't much." With a Dutch surname, I always felt comfortable as a member of this church. Yet, our church was different from most other churches in the denomination. While we were still predominantly white and middle class, our church sat smack dab in the middle of a working class neighborhood of color. It wasn't always so. Originally the area had indeed been home to many white, middle class families, but time and city growth changed everything.

As a youth, I can remember serious attempts by the church to interact with the community and to draw them in. Occasionally, these attempts showed a modicum of success, but more often the efforts produced marginal effects. Shortly after I graduated from high school and moved from the area, so, too did the church of my youth. The building was sold and the church moved to the comforts of the suburbs where it continues to this day.

As inner city churches face the continuing dilemma of shrinking membership and declining numbers of inner city churches, one must stop and ponder several key questions.

- For a church to survive, must it be necessary to leave the inner city and replant itself in a more compatible setting?
- For a new church plant to succeed, must we always look to the suburbs for locations in which to plant the seeds of the Gospel?
- For any church to survive and grow, must we seek out membership that will be of a similar culture, ethnicity, or social status?

Based the Bible's instruction to the church, I believe our answer must be an unequivocal and resounding NO! At this juncture in the life of the church, I believe that we must turn to the scriptures now more than ever for instruction and guidance. With that in mind, I believe that the Bible spells out the following truths for us to claim, reflect upon, and then use as a basis for future action…

- God's message of salvation is for all people, regardless of who they are where they come from, how much they earn or where they live. For proof of this tenet, please see Acts 10:9-11:18, where we read of Peter's vision, ensuing journey to the house of Cornelius and the reaction of the Apostles to the preaching of the Gospel to the Gentiles. We must also review the events of Acts 8:26-40 and Philip's call to preach to the Ethiopian.
- Secondly, we must recognize that within the church, there can be no preferential treatment or division of people. For support review Paul's instructions to the church in Corinth in I Corinthians 4:6-7, where Paul states, "For what makes you different from anyone else? What do you have that you did not receive?"
- Everything we have, and everything we are is a gift from God! It is not ours. We did not earn any of it. It is all a gift of God! We do not own it. Turning to Ephesians 4:4, Paul

reminds the Ephesians that there is "one body and one Spirit." We all serve the same God. Let us pull together and begin to act as a single body rather than a disjointed collection of unconnected bones reminiscent of Ezekiel's valley of dry bones recorded in Ezekiel 37.

- Finally, we must remember that it is not the work of God's people to build God's church. Our duty is to preach the Gospel, sharing the Good News. God is in the business of building His Church. Don't believe me? According to Mark 16:15 we are commanded to "go into all the world and preach the good news to all creation." Or, read Christ's final words to his disciples in Acts 1:8, "You shall be my witnesses in Jerusalem, and in all Judea and Samaria and to the ends of the earth."

The challenge facing the church today is the same challenge that Peter and the Apostles faced. We all know that we are to reach out into all communities, but somehow we haven't personally accepted the same charge from God. Consequently, we find it easier and more comfortable to associate with those most similar instead of breaching the gap and joining hand-in-hand in prayer, in unity, and in worship with those who are different from us.

Yes, the church can survive in the inner city. In fact, the church can survive anywhere God has decided to build His church. We must quit running and respond with love to everyone whom God calls!

Life in the Fast Food Lane

"Be still before the LORD and wait
patiently for him." (Psalm 37:7)

McDermit's seemed difficult to get into these days. Every time Ernie stopped in there seemed to be more and more people had chosen to eat at his favorite restaurant. Some days he thought he would never find a parking spot. Today had been one of those days. Ernie had circled the building at least three times before finally spotting a young family piling into their van. Ernie pulled up and waited patiently for the family to get settled and pull away. He slid quickly into the remote parking space that had just been vacated.

With a clear view of the main dining area as well as the drive-up window, Ernie quietly turned off the ignition and sat back for a moment. Relaxing in the quiet of the car and bopping to the music of his favorite oldies song, Ernie observed the hustle and bustle of the tiny restaurant that had become sort of his kitchen away from home.

The song ended, but Ernie made no effort to move. Ernie watched silently as countless families continued to come and go. Almost as many people walked out with bags of fast food as those who drove through the drive-up window. Dinner had become just another meal on the run for America's families.

Ernie tapped on the power door locks. The locks snapped up.

Leisurely, he opened the door and slid from the comfort of the Lincoln. Immediately, the noise of the restaurant traffic accosted him.

Entering the building, the crowd was larger than he expected and the noise far more deafening. The constant "beep, beep, beep" of the deep-fat fryers was barely audible above the chatter of children noisily playing in the large indoor playground. It was unlikely that any of the patrons were truly able to carry on a decent conversation, but it was evident that many were trying.

After reviewing the options before him, Ernie took his place in line. Slowly he progressed to the front.

"Hamburger, fries and a small coffee," he requested. The order had become almost a nightly ritual.

Quickly recognizing a regular, the teen behind the counter barely nodded before zipping away to hurriedly fill the order. She returned burger and fries in hand. "For here?" she queried, as she reached down for a tray. She knew the answer before Ernie even had a chance to respond. "That'll be $4.56, please."

Ernie handed her a five-spot, and accepted his change. Turning, he struggled past the other waiting patrons, settling into a corner from which he could observe the comings and goings in the sea of strangers.

"How did we ever get to this point?" Ernie mused. He understood why he always ate out. As a recent bachelor, he hated eating alone, but it was even tougher at home. At least when he ate out he had the sense of being accompanied for dinner - even if it was a bunch of bouncing kids in the next booth. But how could all the families so willingly give up the quiet solitude of home and the closeness of meals eaten in lively conversation?

The answer would wait for another time as Ernie gulped down the last of his food and gave a furtive glance at his watch.

"Oh, no! It's already 6:30. I'm supposed to be at the kids' school meeting by now!"

Quickly Ernie picked up his trash, stuffed it into the bin by the door and hurried out.

Author's Insight: Get It Now!

Our society has become dependent on *instant* or *fast* items. Many of us arise in the morning to take a quick shower, followed by an instant breakfast drink. For lunch, if we bother to stop at all, it is another quick meal from a fast-food restaurant. By the time we get off work, we are too tired to cook, so we throw another frozen dinner in the microwave or grab one more fast food item from the drive through.

However, we want more than just our food fast. We enjoy too fast cars and fast music. (When was the last time you really slow-danced a whole night away?) We move fast in romance, which is often followed by a quickie divorce. Even in our intimacy, we long for instant gratification, as we are too busy to get to know one another or to hold each other in a prolonged embrace. We grow impatient for a 45-second traffic light.

The glory days of long walks, relaxing bicycle rides, and slow moving trains may be gone forever. They all take too long. Instead, we hop in the car to *run* to the corner convenience store. We jump aboard a jet to save a three-hour drive. A recent advertisement for a national physical fitness center even boasted that we could get a full hour's workout in only thirty minutes!

Volumes have been written about how our society has progressed (or regressed) to our present predicament. Causes are as varied as the authors who wrote them. Some say that we are merely the products of our technologically advanced society. Others propose that we have forgotten our God. In our quest for total satisfaction, we search feverishly, forever racing from one activity to another. As I see it, to expound on the causes really sidesteps the true question, "What have we lost in our ferver, in our constant rush?"

I propose there are, indeed, many valuable that we have lost on the way. Actually, some actions are better lost than retained. However, several desirable characteristics have also been cast aside. Many have lost the ability to contemplate in quiet solitude. Some have lost the enjoyment of the beauty of nature. Most have lost the art of true communication and have forgotten what communicating with

God truly entails. We are out of step with ourselves, with nature, with others, and with God.

Unable to sit in quiet solitude, we are not in touch with who we truly are or what we truly feel. One of the greatest literary works of all time, Henry David Thoreau's <u>Walden Pond</u>, is marvelous work gathered from hours of quiet contemplation. Because of changes in our society, we are no longer free to repeat the works of his masterpiece. Indeed, many have never heard his words, much less experienced them. Until one can sit awhile and reflect, they will never be able to say with conviction that perhaps we too "march to the beat of a different drummer."

Arguably the greatest twentieth-century American poet was Robert Frost. Frost was renowned for his wonderful, poetic sketches of nature. As children, many baby boomers learned to recite the words to Frost's now famous "Two Roads." Vincent Van Gogh, the modern-day Dutch painter, was also famous for his mastery in putting nature to the canvas. It is my contention that all of us must first learn to accept and appreciate nature before we can learn to communicate with others.

The process of communicating with others is now a lost art. We greet each other in the store or in our churches with the classic cliché, "Hi, how are you?"

Yet, rarely do we really want the answer. Many often do not even pause long enough for the person to even politely respond, "Fine." Many can no longer sit to discuss a good book, even the least divisive conversation two people could share. Most would be hard pressed to admit they know their neighbors, which is a shame. What an even greater shame that we no longer are able to intimately converse with even our families. The days of meaningful conversation around the dinner table have been replaced with running to and fro or watching television.

An extremely influential early Christian author (The Apostle Paul in Romans 1:20) once wrote, "God's invisible quantities – his eternal power and divine nature – have been clearly seen, being understood from what has been made, so that people are without excuse." The agony of the current situation is that a great number of individuals in our society have lost the ability to recognize God. Others may still recognize Him, but are often at a loss on how to communicate with Him. Our fast-paced society has taught us to push God aside. We do not have time. Consequently, when we do have time, we do not know how. Evidence can be seen by the vast number of books available on the subject of prayer and by the enormous popularity of Sunday School classes on learning to pray.

An early professor of mine at Texas Lutheran College in Seguin, Texas, Dr. August Wenzel, used to chastise his freshman theology classes with the statement that "Man should be under God, beside his brother, in the world." People cannot achieve this impressive correlation of relationships unless they are also in touch with themselves.

The scriptures teach us in Luke 2:52 that "Jesus grew in wisdom and stature, and in favor with God and man." Our society has caused us to misplace our values. Instead of balancing our lives among the four aspects of mental, physical, spiritual and social equality, our fast-paced society has taught us to ignore the balance and go for the moment.

I, for one, have belatedly, learned to step back, and slow down.

The road was not an easy one, brought about through a combination of a life-threatening illness. After visiting a doctor in 1993 for a routine checkup, I was instructed to go immediately to the hospital across the street. Because I was bleeding so badly internally from stress, it was necessary to give me three units of blood before they could even operate. Recovery provided the pause I needed to change directions and reclaim my grasp of solitude and communion with God.

Caution. Speed limit ahead. People communicating - with each other, with themselves, with the world... and with God.

Beth Boese

The Race

"I have fought the good fight, I have finished the race, I have kept the faith." - II Timothy 4:7

Brian literally fell across the finish line exhausted, but at the same time, he was exhilarated. Never in his wildest dreams did he imagine that the sense of accomplishment would feel so great. Months of training led up to this point, and it all started on a dare.

Sitting around a couple of months ago, the close quartet of friends, being typically boys, bragged about the various abilities each possessed. Brian could no longer remember who said it first, but someone halfheartedly suggested the challenge of running a marathon and everyone except Dave quickly responded to the challenge.

Dave simply did not see the sense in the exercise, remarking that it would be a lot of work with no visible benefit. His words still rang in Brian's ear, "What can we gain by learning that we can run a marathon other than to prove what everyone is already saying... that we're just a bunch of jocks?"

In the fervor of the moment, Jim grabbed his Blackberry, connected quickly, and found a local marathon with a date close enough that they would not lose focus, but was also far enough out that they had time to train.

As competent athletes, the high school stars had continued

to shine in their college careers; so the early training proved no challenge. A couple of weeks into the training they began to stretch out the distances that they ran and added off-road work to their regiment.

Although Jim had been the most ardent supporter of the idea, he quickly tired of the routine and began to make excuses why he didn't want to run with them. By the end of the first week, he simply was nowhere to be found.

Pete and Brian kept at it, encouraging each other at every opportunity. Eventually the training became more manageable as their bodies became acclimated to the torture of running twenty-some miles every other day, mixed with a regimen of strength and endurance routines on off-days.

As they progressed, Brian noticed something else happening. Gradually the impetus for training shifted from one of simply wanting to prove he could do it to a real desire to complete the challenge before him. It was no longer about the dare, but the urge to succeed grew, and it became the focal point of his efforts.

Along the way, both boys soon learned that their efforts required a great deal of sacrifice also. The camaraderie they had experienced with Dave and Jim waned. The Friday night partying soon gave way to healthier living. In order to make room for the two- to three-hour training sessions, many of the simple pleasures they had enjoyed were tossed to the wayside like driftwood on the waves.

With less than a week to go before the marathon, Brian faced another shock. Pete announced he was not going to compete. Pete told him that he would be there to support Brian on race day, but he admitted he didn't feel that he was ready for what lay ahead.

"Maybe next time," Pete offered. Both of them knew that there would not be a next time for Pete. Although he had starred in high school sports, college sports had been Pete's Albatross, sapping his confidence slowly.

Finishing the race, Brian crumpled to the pavement, spent. He offered a short prayer, thanking God for allowing him to be able to complete the challenge that seemed so distant just a few short weeks ago.

Gradually Brian's thoughts shifted to thoughts of another race that he remembered his Pastor had spoken about. The Apostle Paul had written about it, but it was one of those passages Brian had trouble relating to in his Christian walk. Run the race... Finishing was the goal...

Now at last he understood what the Apostle Paul meant when he wrote in II Timothy 4:7, "I have fought the good fight, I have finished the race, I have kept the faith."

Author's Insight – Each Has a Unique Gift

At first glance, this story may seem like a retelling of Christ's famous Parable of the Sower. In fact, a strong argument can be made for such an interpretation; yet that is far from the original intent of this tale. Rather, this was intended to be a parable of how many folks operate within the Church.

Some people, like Dave, they are members of the Church but who really have no desire to be actively involved. They are afraid of being classified as outcasts or, in the vernacular of the world, Holy Rollers. When the opportunity for more than cursory involvement surfaces, they are quick to shy away.

Some church members are like Jim. They think the ideas presented in the Church are great and they get behind every new ministry idea yet quickly tire of the regimen required to keep a ministry going. Committee meetings are missed... activities don't get done... and pretty soon they are off chasing something else, completely oblivious of the commitment they made.

Many, too, are those who function within the Church like Pete prepared for the marathon. They are on-board with ministries from the outset and remain faithful for a long time. When the goal is within reach, however, they fall away. The reasons they step aside are numerous, ranging from being afraid of succeeding to simply being wary of being noticed. Their personal desire is to work within the Church – provided no one knows.

Those church members like Brian are few and far between. Few ever realize the exhilaration of completing a task for God or recognizing their own personal growth, which happened while their eyes were focused on God.

Truly, the Church is in need of more Brian-like Christians. The church faces a challenge to raise up more people who have the compassion, the drive, and the fortitude to go the distance for God. Unless the Church finds and trains more Brian-like Christians, we run the risk of alienating society and being on the sidelines when we are needed in the trenches.

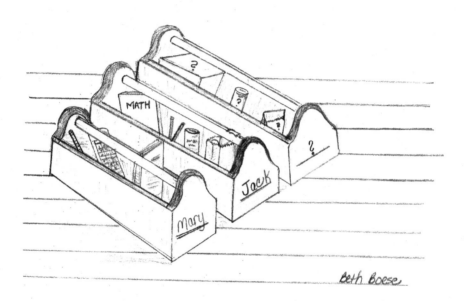

Beth Boese

The Garage

"There are different kinds of gifts, but the same Spirit." (I Corinthians 12:4)

A garage!

It is probably the one thing at that point in my life that I missed most about not living in a house. I used to spend hours in my garage working on various projects. I had even managed to build up quite a collection of tools. Funny thing, though, it seems that every time I used a new tool, it always took me several tries to get it right. Pity the poor recipient of any project that required me to use a new tool!

As I was musing over this idea one day, my mind began to wander. (Daydreaming seems to be an inevitable consequence of quiet time - but that is a thought for another time.) As my mind wandered through myriad thoughts, I suddenly envisioned myself standing in the middle of a very large and beautiful church.

I must have looked terribly awestruck because, before long, I was approached by an impeccably dressed young man.

"This church must take quite of lot of work to keep up," I blurted out. (Just like a dreamer - always thinking about the amount of work involved.)

His response floored me. "No. We have a lot of people willing to try."

He then went on to explain. As new members arrive, each is

given a toolbox with a variety of tools. No one receives the same mix of tools, and no one can receive all of them either. Two rules were strictly enforced. No one could borrow tools they did not have and each is forbidden to lend their tools out. Because many tools are needed for each task, they are encouraged to ask each other for assistance, thereby building each other up.

"Look at Mary over there," he said. "Mary just recently came to us. Prior to her arrival here, Mary had experience with most of the tools in her box. She just was never taught to use them properly. For instance, as a successful businesswoman with lots of responsibility, Mary was well adapted to money management, but for all the wrong reasons. Therefore, one of the tools supplied in Mary's box was a book on sound fiscal policy, dealing with such matters as tithing and setting of priorities."

"Jack, on the other hand, has been with us for quite some time. Jack, for reasons that don't matter anymore, came to us as an experienced house-husband. Man, can that guy entertain! To top it all off, Jack also teaches his children at home - showing a tremendous talent for teaching. In his box, we included a variety of tools essential to hospitality, as well as some to assist him with his teaching endeavors."

"We have made every attempt to suit the tools with the person."

With that, the young man took his leave.

"But, but, but that's not what I meant..." I started to protest. But I realized he probably already knew that.

Suddenly I snapped back to reality.

Now, if you will excuse me - I may not have a garage, but I certainly have some tools that need some use!

Author's Insight - Ready to Volunteer?

America is in trouble and sinking fast.

Now that I have your attention, perhaps I should be prepared to back up what I say. America was founded as a nation bent on providing religious freedom for persecuted Christians around the world. The "Protestant work ethic" is what helped build this nation into a strong, vibrant nation - a nation where people wanted to come and build new lives. Neighbors helped neighbors. Everyone pitched in to make a community work. Even our churches were full of people ready to help out, making ministries run smoothly, and making an impact on the community around them.

Sadly, I think those days are behind us. Why? A better question perhaps would be, "Do we have to be this way?"

Let me answer the first question as a lead in to the second and more basic question. I believe we have left the days of the Protestant work ethic and volunteerism behind us because we have lost our foundational belief in God. Many people in the United States sincerely believe in God. Yet, they do not believe that He is active in our country; and they surely do not believe that He takes an active interest in their personal lives. That's too bad. The God I love considers me as His son (see Galatians 4:7). As a father, I know that I am always concerned with what is happening in the lives of my children, even when they don't see me actively involved, I am concerned for their very well-being. Consequently, to leave God out of our lives deprives us of the best source of strength and inspiration one could ever hope to have.

When we leave God out of our lives, it isn't long before we begin to look inward and become self-centered. With a self-centered outlook on life, we begin to lose the desire to help others. We begin to worry more about our own survival as individuals than our survival as a community.

But, must we stay this way?

In a nutshell, no. But it will take some work on our part. I believe that we can reverse the process, but it needs to start now and needs to begin with each person.

What needs to change? I am glad you asked! Being an optimist, I am always looking for solutions for problems instead of simply analyzing them.

1. We must begin with a clear concept of God's teaching, "Men shall know us by our fruits." We cannot expect others to see God in us and active in our lives if we do not exhibit the same type of fruit that Christ Jesus exhibited. He loved and cared enough for us that he sacrificed his very life for our salvation.

2. We must follow that concept up with a clear plan of action. Each person God has placed on this earth is unique. God has given to each of us different abilities and talents. We must determine what our talents are, and how to effectively use them for the general welfare of those around us. We can make that determination by imagining we have a compass for our lives. Each direction points us to another source of God's wisdom:

   North: ask for our Neighbor's counsel.
   East: examine the Events in our lives.
   South: listen to the Spirit of God active in our lives.
   West: explore the Word of God.
   All directions must be searched in a spirit of Prayer.

3. We must act and act decisively. The time is too far gone to make meager attempts at change. We must act now. We must act courageously. We must act out of love.

If each person who claims to know God begins to act on these concepts, this country, and our churches, would change drastically. Remember, James has already made it plain, "Faith without works is dead" (James 2:17). Let us begin to act now before our country and our churches are beyond saving.

Beth Boese

A Still Small Voice

"After the earthquake came a fire, but the Lord was not in the fire. And after the fire came a gentle whisper."(I Kings 19:12)

With dinner over and the kids off playing, Chuck plopped into his favorite easy chair while his wife, Melinda, finished the dishes. Another long day, in a string of exhausting days, often left him seeking the comfort of his chair early in the evening. Tonight was no exception as Chuck looked forward to escaping the pressures of his busy life.

Grabbing the remote, he quickly found his favorite news and picked up the book he had been reading. Accustomed to multi-tasking throughout the day, juggling the TV and a book was normally little challenge. The combination quickly provided the soothing escape Chuck so desperately sought. Barely a few moments had passed before Melinda heard the snoring emanating from the living room.

Chuck frequently napped in the evenings throughout their marriage. Chuck called them is power naps and he claimed they were needed to refresh him for the evening. Early in their marriage, his evening naps had bothered Melinda; but in recent years, she had come to appreciate them because they reminded her he was home with her and comfortable in their life.

Lately, however, Chuck's napping had taken on a different dimension. They were more frequent and often lasted much longer.

On many occasions he simply woke from his nap just in time to retire for the night.

As he dozed, Chuck began to dream of lush countryside, resplendent in a kaleidoscope of colorful blossoms and rushing waters. Chuck startled when he heard a strange roaring noise that he did not recognize, almost as if all of nature itself had begun calling his name. He tried to move as if to respond to the sounds, but he found he could not. He tried to speak, but was unable to utter even a muted, hoarse whisper.

Frantic, his mind began to race. He did not understand what was happening; he felt trapped and frustrated at his inability to respond.

Just as quickly as it started, the dream ended and Chuck bolted upright in his chair.

Hearing the noise of his movements, Melinda entered the living room. Chuck was nearly white, almost as if he had seen a ghost. "What's wrong, Honey?" she implored.

Dreaming was a rarity for Chuck, and it was even rarer still to recall what he dreamt. This time was different. He vividly remembered every aspect of his dream and his inability to respond. As he explained the dream to Melinda, the same sense of dread and frustration welled up inside him.

Half-jokingly, Melinda replied, "Maybe God is trying to get your attention."

While she had replied somewhat in jest, Melinda was keenly aware of the ways that God chooses to get the attention of His people. She had been there too often herself, allowing the busyness of life to slide her away from God. But then unexplainable events would occur, which jostled her back to God.

Neither spoke of the dream again that evening, not even as they put the kids to bed nor turned in for the evening themselves. After a rushed time of devotion and prayer, Chuck laid his head on the pillow and began to drift off to sleep in the now quiet house.

As he drifted, Chuck began to dream again of the peaceful hills and vibrant meadows he envisioned earlier. In the solitude of the night, rather than the roaring of nature, Chuck heard a still small voice gently call to him.

Willingly, yet feebly, as if remembering his wife's admonishment, Chuck responded, "Yes Lord?"

His thoughts turned to thoughts of God, and of peace, and of tranquility.

Author's Insight: Time Out!

All too often, we find ourselves busier than we expect or plan to be. Unfortunately, when we find ourselves in such situations, one of the first things that fall by the wayside is our relationship with God, which is actually the last thing that should suffer.

When we stray in our walk with God because of the busyness in life, God can and does use unusual means to grab our attention. Sometimes God will get our attention through the words, or actions, of others. Occasionally God will use events in our lives to turn our attention to him.

I speak from experience when I say that God can and will use nature to get our attention. I have marveled at the wonders of God's handiwork in the rush of a mountain stream and in the delicate beauty of fragrant wildflowers. I have witnessed His majesty in the brewing storm clouds and in the stillness of a winter snowfall.

Those times when I most sense God's presence frequently occur when I have managed to stray from a close walk with Him because of the hustle and bustle of life.

Keeping communication open with God is a difficult task in the hustle and bustle of life, but one in which the benefits far outweigh the effort. Often, however, it is simply a matter of priorities.

According to Taylor Gandossy (2009), Nielsen - the noted ratings firm - reports the average person spends more than 151 hours per month in front of the television. Christina Warren (2009) reports the average US consumer spends an additional 68 hours per month online. Neither of these figures account for time spent on the phone, in either text messaging or conversation. Likewise, these figures do not account for time spent attending theater events, school functions, sporting events, or simply goofing off.

It does not take advanced mathematics to figure out that the average American is spending more than five hours per day on voluntary, mind-numbing leisure activities.

God has called each of us to give a tithe. Few would argue that a tithe is appropriate from our incomes, although some debate rages about whether our tithe applies to our gross incomes or net incomes. Yet, relatively few consider that our tithe also should be applied to our time and talents.

If we have more than five hours per day that we can spend in front of electronic devices that do little more than numb our minds to the events of the world, imagine the difference a tithe of our time could make. Imagine tithing two and a half hours per day to God. What difference do you think it would make in our individual lives, our outlook on life, our spiritual growth, and the advancement of God's kingdom?

The differences could be staggering!

Not only would our churches have ample volunteers, but the amount of Biblical knowledge would increase, while the influence of the world on Christians would dramatically decrease.

What will it take for you to find the time to devote to God?

Beth Boese

Nostalgia Lane

"A new command I give you: Love one another.
As I have loved you, so you must love one another.
By this everyone will know that you are my disciples,
if you love one another" (John 13:34-35)

I took a trip the other day down Nostalgia Lane, a quiet, little street just like many found in most towns. Except, this lane's peculiar attributes distinguish it from any other street I have ever seen. For openers, two people walking down this same street will see completely different paths. Funny, even as I walked down, and then back, I noticed that the lane seemed different, even to me. Another strange phenomenon is this street's size. A quick glance down the lane makes one feel as if it is, indeed, a very short street. However, as one wanders, the street never seems to end.

As the name hints, this street offers one a very unique view back into the past, but not just any past, only particulars which strollers along the lane have been intimately involved.

As I tarried on my stroll, stretches of Nostalgia Lane seemed to take longer to pass, with more and more events occupying the same spots. Rounding the curve of another year, I observed the street seem to lengthen. In fact, others have reported that the older you become the longer this lane will be. This amazing street revealed the impact it has had on my life. As I meandered down the pathway, every step reminded me of places I had seen, people I had known, and things I had done.

Continuing on my way, I found that many of those events, of which I had just been reminded, bore a great deal of cause and effect on the events which appeared later on my journey.

On my trip down the lane, I found several jewels which I will carry with me for the rest of my life. I did not have time to tarry, but some items simply could not be left behind.

The first jewel which I found closely resembles a ruby, a deep, precious red gemstone, which only a few can truly enjoy. This jewel is the gift of salvation offered through the blood of Christ. Anyone who asks receives this jewel. It is not deserved. Often, it is neglected. However, this gem is eternal. In faith, I bowed down to receive this jewel.

As I continued, I picked another jewel from the ground. Although this gemstone resembled a pearl, it was not extravagant. This pearl-like ball was not even perfect. It more closely resembled the type of pearls found in a five-and-dime. It was a cultured pearl; the common man's jewel. The gem will be a most precious treasure for me; it is the jewel of knowledge, no of wisdom. It optimizes wisdom garnered from a lifetime of experiences. While knowledge can be taught, wisdom must be learned through one's own experiences. As I discovered, true wisdom only comes through once one has grabbed onto faith, for it is only then that the experiences of life truly gain meaning. Wisdom can only be retrieved in hope, hoped offered through salvation.

Yet a third jewel I encountered resembled a diamond. A stone, which had been tried by fire, crushed under the weight of neglect, tossed aside in the busyness of life, and, yet, the jewel of true friendship still sparkles. It awaits reclamation. But the diamond-like gem can only be reclaimed by one to whom it originally belonged. With love, I stooped and picked it up. Yet, without faith and without wisdom, friendship is merely companionship.

Yet, of all of the jewels I found, the most precious jewel in my chest and which I will carry always is the jewel of love. A jewel against which there is no comparison, it is among the most precious stones and resembled rare Alexandrite, changing colors to match the light of surrounding friendships. As I observed along my walk, the more I shared this gem freely with those I passed, the greater my own stone grew.

As I walked, I plucked these jewels from the ground. I wondered who could have been so careless as to discard these precious gems. It was then I realized that this was my street. I had let these fall.

Have you found your jewels yet?

Author's Insight – When You See Life Passing By

In the hustle and bustle of everyday living, we may lose sight of the things that matter, like our friends, our family, our personal well-being, and our walk with God. Often, we replace these with temporary things that cloud our judgment or simply bring temporary happiness.

This story sprang from a Bible study I attended at one time, where we were discussing the various fruits of the Spirit: love, joy, peace, patience, goodness, kindness, gentleness, faithfulness, and self-control. We were talking about how often many of these fruits directly affect our relationships with others, when several of us simultaneously realized that even those who claim to be devout Christians often have not grasped the message, or made use of these fruits in their lives. From there the essence of the story was born.

We get so caught up in the busyness of life that we forget what is truly important. Only when we pause, and take stock of our lives, do we discover the gems we might be missing along the way. We see the events of our lives unfold before us and wonder, "How could I have been so blind."

But we do not have to be so blind!

Walking with the Spirit of God truly alive in our lives nurtures these gems to where they spring forth. While they make take time for them to develop, we must also put forth effort under God's total control.

We cannot simply give God control of part of our lives and expect these gems to blossom. We need to give Him complete control. The Bible teaches, in Luke 2:52, that Jesus developed in four distinct areas: physically, mentally, socially, and spiritually. We cannot focus exclusively on one area without one of the other aspects of our lives suffering. We must take care of our bodies for they are the "temple of the Holy Spirit." We must be mentally challenge ourselves, because we must be prepared to answer anyone who might ask us about the reasons for the joy we possess. We must grow socially, because the "one another" phrases of the New Testament give us no option. More than 40 times, the New Testament commands us to do something for one another. From loving one another, to encouraging one another, to holding one another accountable, all require social interaction. Finally, we must be spiritually growing, because it will prepare us for what God has in store for our lives.

Do not waste your time allowing life to pass you by. Grasp it firmly in the manner in which God intended for us to enjoy it.

Beth Boese

A Time to Heal

*"He heals the brokenhearted
and binds up their wounds." (Psalms 147:3)*

Richard's mind wandered as he drifted in and out of the anesthesia, waiting for the full effects to take hold.

It seemed like only yesterday that he had been to see Dr. Maxim for a check-up. The doctor had pronounced Richard healthy, but he need to start taking a little better care of himself before it was too late. Although he hated to admit it, the doctor was probably right. He had always felt himself to be invincible, and tenaciously followed the doctor's orders, for a while. Soon he was too busy living to worry about a healthy diet, proper exercise, and plenty of sleep.

Richard wondered how long it had been since that doctor's visit. One year? Maybe two? Perhaps longer? He simply couldn't remember.

And now this.

Richard began to succumb to the deepening effects of the anesthesia. Before he fell headlong into the induced slumber, he tried to remember the events which caused him to be lying on this operating table. The recollections were vague. Perhaps because of the anesthesia or perhaps because of the trauma, but the last twenty-four hours seemed to be a hazy blur.

Richard had gone to a party with some friends. They were celebrating the arrival of a much needed new business in town.

Everyone thought it would be a great addition to the community. With the gala, there were introductions, toasts, and well wishes everywhere. It was a big occasion. Sometime during the evening's events, Richard began to experience a burning pain in his chest. It felt like nothing he had ever experienced before. Then, just as quickly it dissipated. Richard remembered making a mental note to himself to get it checked out.

That was the last memory Richard was absolutely sure about.

He vaguely recalled the ambulance ride. As the sirens wailed their warning, Richard could hear the screams of his wife as she witnessed what was happening to her husband, and to her. He vaguely recalled someone beating on his chest and the beep-beep-beep of the monitor which someone quickly attached. As he was wheeled into the hospital, he recalled people running in every direction. At least, he thought he remembered the big picture. The details were gone as everything seemed to blur together.

As Richard's mind drifted deeper into the effects of the anesthesia, he mentally noted the room around him and he took a few stealthy glances of his surroundings. There seemed to be a never-ending assortment of machines, each beeping out their messages. The lights were far brighter than anything he could recall, and they were all directed on him. He was the star, or at least the star patient.

Among the machines and the lights, a sea of people readied for surgery, each absorbed into their individual tasks. Struggling to recall, he noticed a couple of nurses fidgeting with some equipment in the corner. The anesthesiologist seated by his head, carefully measured the proper dosage of medicine to put him under. One doctor he noted was the big, somber-faced doctor beside a tray of silvery tools. This man simply took charge of the room, constantly barking orders to others while still maintaining concentration on his own tasks.

The surgery took longer than expected, but Richard had been put deep into the clutches of induced sleep. Doctors and nurses hummed alongside each other in a concert of harmonic medicine. Richard's heart had suffered severe damage. If and when Richard recovered, he would face a long and arduous journey back to health. Seven hours into the surgery, the conductor issued the cue the orchestra had waited for. "Let's close him up." Those words were a simple but fitting climax to a masterful production.

"Richard." A soft voice called him from his slumber.

There it was again. "Richard." Concentrating on the voice, Richard used every ounce of strength to turn toward the voice. "Richard, I love you. You're going to be all right. Honey, please let me know you hear me," the voice continued.

Richard struggled to respond. It had been a long ordeal. Slowly he managed a weak smile.

Richard had faced the brink of death and he knew it. He also realized that without everyone who had worked so closely together, he would not be here now.

"I love you." Richard had difficulty with the words and was not even sure he spoke them, but he thought he did. "Tell them thanks." That was all he could muster. Exhausted, Richard succumbed to drugs. Only time would tell if indeed he would, indeed, be all right.

Author's Insight: You Are the Temple of the Holy Spirit

Illness is a fact of life. The chances of falling seriously ill rise exponentially as you grow older. Increasingly, people have rushed to search for the solution to aging, either through the doctor's office, a pharmacist, or a gym. Everyone seeks to find the hidden Fountain of Youth.

Yet, one must ask why so many are slow to rise from the slumber into reality. Why do we worship at the altar of the all-you-eat-buffets or lounge in the all-day pajamas in front of the idiot box? Every moment we waste, delaying before moving to health and fitness is another moment lost that cannot be recovered.

While most folks may choose to change, perhaps at a snail's pace, not all do. While such delays continue to destroy your health (and ultimately your pocket book as well), the reality is that it does not have to be that way. In fact, I would argue that for the Christian, it must never be that way. Simply put, the Bible tells us in I Corinthians 6:19 that we are "temples of the Holy Spirit." As a result, we are to honor and glorify God with our physical bodies. How can we follow this tenet of Christian life if we do nothing to care for our bodies?

Yes, you might assume that I am "the last one to talk." In 2011, you might have been right. But then I decided to do what was right and make the changes necessary to take better care of my body. I have lost more than 70 pounds, eliminated caffeine, improved my heart health and rid myself of both cholesterol and high blood pressure medication. In addition, I have begun a walking regiment that truly makes most pause.

In 2014, I walked from Oklahoma to Nebraska. In 2015, I traversed Kansas the other direction, walking from Missouri to Colorado. In 2018, Lord willing, I will hike from Seattle to Miami.

Yes, I was an obese, medically dependent person who failed to bring glory to God in my body. All of that has changed. Now I can say TO GOD BE THE GLORY.

Beth Boese

One Last Field

"The glory of young men is their strength,
gray hair the splendor of the old." – Proverbs 20:29

A bit misty-eyed, Bart gazed out over the field that spread before him as he realized this was the last field to be harvested in a career that spanned more than 60 years. Nearing 80, he had begun his life as a farmer while still a teenager helping his father harvest this very field. For this reason, he had saved this quarter to be the final one.

As he sat motionless in the tractor, Bart's mind wandered from recollections of past years to the days that lay ahead, wondering what he would do now. After all these years, he had become one with the fields – it was who he was and, in so many ways, what he was.

He recalled years when the crops were lean because of a lack of rain or infestations of disease and pests that he had been unable to control. Often times during those years, they had wondered how they would make it, but, as a man of God, he trusted that God would pull them through and God had always provided for him and his family.

Bart also reminisced about the years when harvests had been so bountiful that wheat and corn were piled on the ground because there was no room in the elevator. Those had been some wonderful years. Those were the rare opportunities that the family had a real vacation. Bart had always made sure to remember that it was God who provided during those years too.

Things had changed so much during the years. Bart recalled the early days, working a harvest in the heat on an old tractor that broke down more than it ran, operating with none of today's modern conveniences like radios and cell phones and air conditioning. They worked from sunup to sundown struggling to get the fields in on time.

Now, with modernized equipment, harvests were almost over before they started because they were not limited to simply daylight hours. For many of his friends, harvests were something you simply paid for by hiring custom cutters. Bart had stood firm that he would harvest his own fields has long as God allowed him the ability to do so.

Alice, his wife of nearly 60 years, had stood by him every step of the way, rarely complaining, always supportive. He had no idea how he would have survived were it not for her. She did so much around the farm too, making sure that tasks were completed that others overlooked – even things that he overlooked.

Alice had never wanted a career in farming, but her love for him overcame that early resistance. She had turned out to be a Godsend. She often knew what he was thinking long before he even said it. The one thing that meant more to Bart than anything, though, was that Alice truly shared his love for God. She shared the same belief that it was God who had always seen them through.

Looking forward, Bart wondered what he would do now that he had decided it was time to give up the one thing that kept him going. The very thought of days with nothing to do scared him more than anything in the world. What would keep him going?

Chirp. Chirp. Chirp.

The sound rang through his thoughts and brought Bart back into reality. He leaned forward and plucked the electronic marvel from its customary location in a pocket on the tractor door.

"Grandpa, you okay?" the voice inquired. It was Bart's oldest grandson.

His grandson had been named after him, but everyone called him Chip. At 28, Chip was the family's hope for the next generation to keep alive the family farm. Chip and his wife Tina had settled into a house next door to Bart and Alice and loved the land as much as they did.

"Yeah, I'm okay," Bart replied. "I was just thinking about... Aw, never mind. I'm okay. I'll see you at the end of the ride."

Bart hung up the receiver, thanking God for providing one more time.

Author's Insight – A New Generation

One of the harsh realities of life is that each of us will grow older. With advancing age, we will be forced to give up many of the things that we have become accustomed to doing for our entire lives. Indeed, many have learned to define the worth of an individual by what they can provide. Once they are no longer able to participate, it is time to cast them aside.

In Proverbs, Solomon gives an alternate message. He states, in a manner of speaking, that gray hair is something that has been earned and carries with it an earned respect. The Apostle Paul even warns Timothy in I Timothy 5:1 to treat older men as his very own father, worthy of respect not harsh rebuke.

Many of the men I have known throughout my life have worked hard and relatively few want to slip quietly away into retirement. This is particularly accurate for true men of God who continue to offer the wisdom of their years. It is an option they should embrace, for they have earned that privilege.

There have been several in my life worthy of note and all bore the same noteworthy trait – they all wanted to provide the younger generation with a better life than what they had experienced. Often this was through the passing of a family farm, but more frequently it was a desire to pass along a deep seated faith in God.

This particular story was written as I observed a friend of mine in western Kansas prepare to pass along the family farm to the next generation. It was a bittersweet moment for him, but as I watched, I saw a bond between my friend and his son develop that was unique.

His son considered his wisdom carefully with each decision. My friend looked forward to being able to spend more precious time with his grandkids, but it did not make it any easier.

What strengthened his ability to cope was the respect his son had for him and his deep faith. May each family strive to preserve the heritage, particularly heritages of faith, from generation to generation.

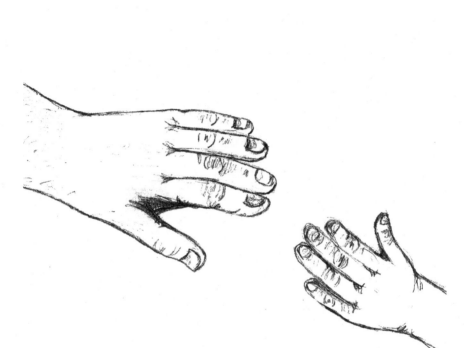

Beth Boese

Just Trust Me!

*"Therefore, if you are offering your gift at the altar
and there remember that your brother or sister has
something against you, leave your gift there in front
of the altar. First go and be reconciled to them; then
come and offer your gift." (Matthew 5:23-24)*

Derrick could still hear his father's words ringing in his ear. The words had been so commonplace in their home that most of the family long ago thought it comical and simply dismissed them. Yet, every time he uttered those words, Derrick's dad was ultimately right. Things worked out for the better.

The first time Derrick remembered hearing those words was when he was just a young boy, and his dad decided it was time for the training wheels to go. Derrick was not ready, not by a long shot – at least in his mind. Yet, his dad persisted.

As Dad ran alongside Derrick's bike he said calmly, "Just trust me." Then, with a swift push, he let go of the bike. Derrick recalled feeling frightened, but then realized he was riding on his own! He remembered the exhilaration as a whole new world opened before him.

Time and time again, Derrick would hear those same words as his father worked with him in improving just about any sporting activity that Derrick pursued. His dad would offer instruction, gentle correction, and with each piece of advice offer the same admonition, "Just trust me!"

When Derrick was ready to get married, but unsure of himself, he asked his Dad for advice. After expounding at length about how a husband should always consider his wife first, which means putting her interests ahead of his own, Derrick heard those familiar words, "Just trust me!"

Who was he to argue? His parents had been married for nearly 40 years, and not once had Derrick heard them argue.

Eventually, things caught up with Derrick and he grew tired of the phrase, which he had begun to consider trite. The two drifted apart. Derrick settled out of town and only came home when absolutely necessary. And he always dreaded hearing those familiar words.

Derrick's chosen separation with his dad had also caused a rift between himself and his mother, but even more so with his sister. He loved them dearly, but simply could not understand how they could put up with the old man's condescending attitude. More than he could bear, Derrick chose to keep his distance. He missed a lot. And, he had to admit, he had also caused them to miss out on so much as well.

Nearly three weeks had passed now since Derrick received the frightening call.

"Derrick, you need to come home," his mother begged. "Your father has had a massive heart attack. They don't know if he'll pull through, or what kind of a life he will have if he lives."

His sister grabbed the phone from their mother and explained, in more detail, about the circumstances. She pleaded with him to hurry.

Finally, when Derrick walked into the hospital room where his father lay, he was ill-prepared for the scene that lay before him. Between the various tubes and monitors, the man in the bed before him hardly resembled the rudy man Derrick remembered. Despite his dread of the phrase, he almost longed to hear those words once more.

Slowly, his father's eyes blinked open. A faint smile crossed his lips and a glimmer shown from the old man's darkened, recessed eyes.

"Dad, I came as quick as I could!" Derrick blurted, reaching to hug his father. Impossible to overcome years of separation in a few moments, Derrick succumbed to the tears, which flowed freely down his cheeks.

And then he heard it!

Reaching with every ounce of energy he had, his Dad patted Derrick and whispered quietly, "Just trust me, Derrick. It will be all right."

Later that evening, Derrick's father passed quietly with the family huddled around.

The time since had been a blur. From the funeral arrangements to dealing with the estate, to simply reminiscing, the entire family had been in constant motion and connection. The years of separation gently washed away in memories of happy times, and floods of tears from tired eyes.

Derrick remembered, sitting back in his chair, and sighed heavily.

"Yes, Dad, I trust you. It will be all right."

Author's Insight – In Our Father's House

This story came about because a former acquaintance went through the agonizing loss of his father, under difficult circumstances, at a time when they were estranged. The agony he suffered was hard to fathom. While I was in my early 20s and still young, I thought I knew enough about death to know that it is permanent and heart wrenching.

I knew that both my friend and his father were believers, which meant I was at a loss as to what to say because of the circumstances until an idea struck me. Truly, things were going to be all right. My friend had lost his father, but not forever. While they would not meet again on this earth, a heavenly reunion awaited them, a reunion that would be unencumbered by the burden of sin.

As I reflected on those circumstances this story began to unfold, but it also began to take on a new meaning in my life. Abandoned as a child and completely bereft of any relationship with my birth parents, circumstances left me with a burning issue. Was it okay to simply continue on the path I found myself treading or did I need to make amends somehow?

Adding to my dilemma, I had become a man I did not recognize nor enjoy being. I was not brought up to be an alcoholic, nor did I grow up learning that abuse (in any form) was acceptable. What was it about my past, and my birth parents, that left me adrift on the Sea of the Unknown?

I had to find out!

I began a quest to find my birth family, a quest that is perhaps better told under different circumstances, where I can expound on my experience. In October of 1989 my search was successful, first in finding my birth father, and, approximately six weeks later, meeting my birth mother.

The experience of meeting my father, relating everything that I had undergone in the intervening years, and offering my forgiveness was the catharsis I needed. A few, short years later my birth father was gone, killed in a tragic auto accident in northern Michigan. But when he left this world, he left knowing I loved him, and I understood why circumstances had gone the way they had for me.

As I continue to reflect on this experience, I wonder how many relationships remain in shambles because one person, or the other, is too proud, or ashamed, to step forward. It does not have to be that way! The sooner that our relationships are healed, the healthier our lives become.

Our Lord makes it very clear our priority before approaching God's throne of grace is one of forgiveness and restoration in relationships in our lives.

Are the relationships in your world mired in the realities of life? You can, and must, make them whole.

Bibliography

Gandossy, Taylor (2009). TV viewing at an all-time high, Nielsen says. *CNN*. Retrieved Feb. 24, 2010 from http://www.cnn.com/2009/SHOWBIZ/TV/02/24/us.video.nielsen/

Krejcir, R. (2007). Statistics and Reasons for Church Decline. *Church Leadership*. Retrieved April 30, 2015, from http://www.churchleadership.org/apps/articles/default.asp?articleid=42346&columnid=4545

Steffan, M. (2013, July). The Surprising Countries Most Missionaries Are Sent From and Go To. *Christianity Today*. Retrieved April 28, 2015, from http://www.christianitytoday.com/gleanings/2013/july/missionaries-countries-sent-received-csgc-gordon-conwell.html

Warren, Christina (2009). Average Internet user now spends 68 hours per month online. *Mashable.com*. Retrieved Feb. 24, 2010 from http://mashable.com/2009/10/14/net-usage-nielsen/.

My Story

I am a 2013 graduate of Western Governors University, with a Bachelor of Science degree in Business Management. I work full time as a production scheduler and data analyst for Eaton Hydraulics in Hutchinson, where I have been since 2002. With 38 years in Information Technology, I am also frequently called on to perform a variety of programming and data tasks to support our production environment.

I have also been a freelance reporter for a variety of Kansas newspapers for the past 16 years, associated exclusively with the Harvey County Independent (Halstead, KS) since 2006. I have written a monthly column called "Tales from the Prairie" for the Independent since late 2013. But my love of writing goes back more than four decades, including producing a newsletter of short stories for nearly a decade under the "Heaven Bound" and "Prairie Tattler" names.

I believe my life has suited me exceptionally well for a book of short stories on life in general.

I was born in Colorado, but spent most of my early years spread between Michigan, Oklahoma and Texas with only brief stopovers in Colorado. If truth be known, now sixty, I have lived in nearly four dozen homes in two dozen cities in five different states.

I have seen the best that life has to offer as a former VP for a Houston-based software company and I have experienced the worst, living in abject poverty in my birth family. I have always had a penchant for noticing details, a character trait that serves me well in both my reporting and the stories I glean from life.

I was abandoned by my birth parents in spring of 1962, just before my 7th birthday and wound up being a double product of the foster care / adoption system in Michigan. Much like my birth family, my first adoption was a life of abuse and neglect. My second adoption in 1965 has been a rousing success. However, the adoption that matters is my adoption as a child of God in 1966.

Although saved, I was not a good example of how to live a Christian life as I repeated much of my birth father's sins, falling into alcoholism and abuse. I am now sober since March of 1989 and violence free since May of the same year. The path I followed was one that I truly knew nothing about until a tearful reunion with my birth family in October of 1989.

My life has been transformed and I am heartily living for the Lord in every aspect of my life

With myriad projects on my plate, rarely do I stay idle. I am working on my autobiography, a book of poetry, a coffee table picture book of historic Kansas churches, and a compilation of my columns of life in rural Kansas. They say that a photograph is worth a thousand words, but many of my photos also get the thousand-word explanation.

My wife and I also are a "Big Couple" with Big Brothers – Big Sisters of Reno County. I currently serve on the council of the First Church of God in Hutchinson, Kansas. I teach the adult Sunday School class and lead evening Bible study groups. I serve on our audio-visual team, while my wife sings on our church's praise team. I am actively pursuing obtaining my ministerial credentials through the Church of God – Anderson. I also am a member of the Kansas Community Leadership Enterprise in Reno County, charged with identifying ways to reduce high school dropout rates across our county. I serve on the Board of Directors for The HUB (Helping the Underprivileged and Broken), a Hutchinson-based inner city ministry service the underprivileged and broken in Reno County. I routinely serve as a regular chapel speaker for The HUB and my wife and I serve as the worship song leaders.

Along the way, I also walk – a lot. In 2014 I walked across Kansas, from Oklahoma to Nebraska. In the summer of 2015, I tackled Kansas the other way, from Eve, Missouri, to Holly, Colorado, for my 60th birthday. While the effort was intended to be pursued in a singular activity, it was twice interrupted by medical issues. The focus of my 2015 walk was primarily to raise funds for local charities while also allowing charities in other areas to benefit. The particular charities I designated were all family-oriented: Big Brothers / Big Sisters of Reno County, First Call for Help of Reno County, Reins of Hope, and Heart to Heart in Harvey County. For more information regarding my walk across Kansas, check out my Charity Steps page on Facebook (facebook.com/KSCharitySteps).

When I retire in 2018, if the Lord wills, I have a walk from Seattle to Miami scheduled to raise awareness for the need for foster parents and adoption. Then my wife and I plan on tackling long-term volunteer work from sea to shining sea. Somewhere in the mix, we are exploring formation of a gospel ministry with some college friends of Charlcie.

Christ tells us in Luke 12:48 that "From everyone who has been given much, much will be demanded" (NIV). Despite my early childhood, I believe much has been given to me and now it is time for me to give back. I only hope that the Lord tarries long enough for me to serve Him in a way that will cause Him to proclaim, "Well done, my good and faithful servant."

Printed in the United States
By Bookmasters